STACKS, STAMPS, AND SMOKE

A missing ex-libris, a cracked window, a body by the alley door

Copyright © 2025 by Ivy Grant

Cover designed by Azameti Michael

Published by Azameti Michael

All rights reserved. No part of this book may be reproduced, distributed, or transmitted in any form or by any means, electronic or mechanical, including photocopying, recording, or any information storage and retrieval system, without the prior written permission of the publisher, except in the case of brief quotations embodied in critical reviews and certain other non-commercial uses permitted by copyright law.

This is a work of fiction. Names, characters, places, and incidents are either the product of the author's imagination or used fictitiously. Any resemblance to actual persons, living or dead, or actual events is purely coincidental.

For information about this title or to request permission for use, please contact:

greyama70@gmail.com

First Edition, 2025

BOOK ONE
PEPPERMINT CAT BOOKSHOP MYSTERIES

TABLES OF CONTENTS

Chapter 1: Founder's Table
Chapter 2: Window Hairline
Chapter 3: Alley Body

Chapter 4: Guestbook Tells
Chapter 5: Router Page
Chapter 6: Press Feet
Chapter 7: Stamp Bite
Chapter 8: Tote Fiber
Chapter 9: Key Custody
Chapter 10: Till and Time
Chapter 11: Alley Cam
Chapter 12: Gran Remembers
Chapter 13: Alternate Heat
Chapter 14: Hardware Truth
Chapter 15: Stamp Test Live
Chapter 16: The Spare
Chapter 17: Timeline Lock
Chapter 18: Assistant Cracks
Chapter 19: Charges Split
Chapter 20: Shop Reset
ABOUT THE AUTHOR

CHAPTER 1

Founder's Table

Morning asks for lists. I give it one. Unlock, lights to soft, kettle on, front bay curtains to half, cones stacked near the travel aisle because the floor wax from last night still needs an hour to finish curing. I scan the room the way a clerk should. Edges clean. Corners honest. Nothing under anything that should not be there. Peppermint pads in on silent feet and inspects the gap between the rug and the Founder's Table. He pauses, decides the gap is innocent, and leaps to the register to stare at me like a new hire who expects training.

"Hold your comments," I tell him. "We set the table first."

The Founder's Table is not a metaphor. It is a four-by-six oak slab with brass feet and a filmed past in the town paper. People like to press their palms to it and claim they feel history. I like the way it supports weight without squeaks. Today it carries a three-piece exhibit: the town's Founder's Ledger on a sunk cradle, a run of sponsor cards, and the original ex-libris stamp under glass. That stamp is the point. The Chamber sold the event as a reunion of our first mark with its ledger. Everyone promises not to touch and then tries to touch. My hands will take the brunt of the day.

Rafi arrives with a roll of blue tape in his pocket and a list printed in large type. He reads things out loud when he wants me to hear them and agree.

"Intake rules," he says. "One. No off-network devices near the exhibit. Two. Hands off glass. Three. No moving the cradle. Four. No food. Five. If you breathe too hard at the stamp, we point at the sign."

"Add a sixth," I say. "If you need to photograph anything, you shoot through my acrylic, not the naked air."

He nods. He prints the revised sign on the little office laser while I set the cradle. Peppermint hops down to patrol the table legs, tail up, whiskers forward. Texture. He offers nothing useful except morale and time checks, which he delivers through yawns.

Gran arrives with the witness ledger tucked under her arm and a sharp pen. The ledger is a basic bound book with ruled pages and a stamped cat on the cover. She made it because the town has learned with us. When people see her sign, they behave. She sets it on the counter, flips to a fresh page, and writes the date in numbers that would please a surveyor.

"Before we let anyone near it," she says. "We say what the thing is."

"Good morning to you too," I say.

She looks like she did when I was ten and I tried to hide a gum wrapper under a floorboard. Gran does not forget. She does not forgive slop. She grinds coffee like a carpenter squares a door.

Rafi returns with the sign and tapes it to the easel by the table. He adds a second sign at eye level by the front bay. He writes the rule about devices in black marker on a small card and tucks it beside the register. He adjusts the lamps. He tilts one bulb to take glare off the glass. He steps back, crosses his arms, and stares. Rafi cares about light the way I care about paper. He says nothing. I let him work.

I set the acrylic vitrine over the stamp base. The base is a simple wood block with two screws and a flat felt pad. The stamp head, cast iron, sits in a narrow slot cut to keep it stable for show. I lift the head with gloved fingers and check the face under the task lamp, not because I expect damage, but because a check now saves a fight later. The letters read clean. The cat's paw sits where the cut always sits on our town mark. I take a short breath, set the head back, and settle the acrylic lid.

"Key," Gran says.

I pull the small brass key from the cloth pouch. Before the pouch touches the table, I open the side cabinet and bring out a tiny tin marked BA. I tap a touch of barium dust onto a cotton swab and pass the swab across the bow and shoulders of the key. A light veil clings to the metal. Not heavy. Barely there. I blow once through my teeth to lift excess. The dust settles in seam lines. It will transfer a trace if someone lifts the key and sets it down when I do not watch.

Gran watches my hands the way she watches fire.

"You logging that," she says.

I pull a card, write the time, write the word barium on it, and tape the card to the underside of the vitrine where only a clerk will look. The key ring goes in a pocket I never use for anything else. I will feel it all day like a tooth.

Peppermint rubs his face on the leg of the Founder's Table. He assesses the vitrine with narrowed eyes, then sits on his haunches and stares up as if he suspects the glass will jump of its own accord.

"It will not fall," I tell him.

He blinks like an auditor and strolls to the guestbook stand, where he places one paw on the little pen and tests the clip. The pen survives. He yawns.

We set the Ledger cradle, tailor the straps across the gutter, and slide the book into place with the care of a surgeon. It opens to the page people want to see, the day the first library committee wrote down a vote to fund shelves. Six names. A blot where someone got excited and stabbed the nib. A loop on a W that I love more than I love some relatives. I lift the acrylic sheet that will float over the paper like a windshield, set the spacers, lower it slow, and listen for anything that sounds like wrong. Silence.

Gran signs the witness ledger. Her lines are like beams. She writes, "Exhibit set, 8:10 a.m., present GW, LW, RM. Vitrine sealed, key retained by LW. Barium dust applied to key. Glass inspected prior to public."

"Read that back," she says.

I read it back. She nods. She adds one more line. "No one handles objects without clerk present."

"Bless you," I say.

We open the door. The first customer is our mail carrier, off route early, a man who likes maps and honest rules. He stands three feet from the table and does not move until I point to the sign. He reads the rules and says, "Works for me." He looks at the stamp head under glass and the ledger under its float and says, "Looks like a church." He means it as respect.

The second visitor is a pair of tourists with strong shoes and a camera that sticks to their bellies like an extra organ. I point to the sign. They nod, lift the camera, and shoot through the acrylic. I offer a ladder of facts, brief and useful. The stamp lived in the first library cabinet. The ledger recorded patrons who paid in beans when coins ran short. The Chamber held the stamp for years, then returned it for the exhibit today. No, the cat does not stamp the cat. Peppermint chooses to ignore them and climbs to the sill where he can glare at pigeons.

At nine, a volunteer from the Chamber calls. Her voice brightens words that should not be bright.

"Liaison will arrive at ten to greet donors," she says.

"Fine," I say. "We will be ready."

The Chamber liaison is Celeste Rourke. She likes a headline and a microphone. She thinks optics matter more than anything. I think chain of custody matters more than optics. We have lived in the same town for years without setting fire to each other. We will test our luck again.

Rafi brings me a clean microfiber cloth and points at the vitrine where a small streak sits along the front edge. He holds a lamp at angle so the streak glares. I keep my hand steady and wipe once in a straight line. A hairline catches light near the top right corner. It sits like a comet two inches long, shallow, almost nothing, precisely something.

"New," he says.

"Maybe from the storage shelf," I say, then hate myself for using that word. I check the corner with a loupe. The scratch runs from front to back. The shallow end faces the room, the deeper end under the bulb. Direction speaks. I take a photo with the scale card and the morning paper at the edge of the frame. I write a short card. Hairline at 9:12 a.m., front to back, vitrine exterior, right edge. I tape the card under the table lip and put the photo in the binder sleeve.

"Not a risk," Rafi says.

"Not a risk," I say. I log it anyway. Paper saves fights I do not want to have.

The room fills. Donations for the reading garden sit in a little jar with a cat sticker. I move the jar twice to avoid shadows and fingerprints. Gran takes the counter and shepherds credit slips through the till without a single error. She eyes the people who get too close to the acrylic and inhales in a way that moves them back an inch.

At ten on the dot, the door opens and Celeste walks in like a ribbon-cutting. She wears a blazer the color of someone else's pride and a fixed smile with teeth. A Chamber volunteer trails her with a tote that says SUPPORT OUR HERITAGE in clean block letters. The tote has enamel pins near the strap, little stars and a cat that looks too shiny for our scruffy mascot.

"Liora," Celeste says. "Your shop looks photogenic."

"It looks like a shop," I say.

She takes in the table and the vitrine and the ledger and the small crowd that is not small enough for her, then sets her sights on the stamp head under glass. Her eyebrows lift the way eyebrows lift when a person imagines their hand on a thing that is not their hand's to hold.

"We will need some footage," she says. "A small segment where I demonstrate the stamp with a good pull. For optics."

"No," I say.

The room quiets, not because my voice is loud, but because I use the word she hates. No. It rattles her the way a coin rattles a tin.

She laughs in a polite way that means she thinks I am joking. "We will stage it," she says. "No ink. I can mime the motion. The clip plays silent anyway."

"No," I say again. "Chain stands between hands and objects. You can speak beside the glass and say whatever you like. The stamp stays under."

She tilts her head a fraction. Her volunteer adjusts the tote strap and pretends to be invisible. Peppermint jumps to the floor and walks to the table and sits with his back to Celeste like a judge who has already heard the case.

"I have authority from the Chamber," she says. "We are the legal custodians of town artifacts."

"You are a partner on this exhibit," I say. "Our ledger sits with our stamp for one day under my roof. That makes me the clerk of record. No hands on objects without my say. The rules are posted. Gran is witness. The camera is welcome. The stamp does not leave the acrylic. Optics enjoy the sign."

Rafi taps the sign with one finger and then acts as if he never touched anything. He did not need to signal. He enjoys due process like other people enjoy football.

Celeste looks at the hairline scratch near the corner and smiles as if the scratch belongs to her. "The glass has a flaw," she says. "If a donor sees a flaw on camera, they will see neglect."

"The flaw is documented," I say. "Direction noted. It is not in frame unless you lean your lens into the light like a raccoon.

Speak on the left side of the table, please."

She exhales in a way that reads as management. Her volunteer sets the tote near the guestbook and pulls out a small clutch of sponsor pins. The tote brushes the edge of the stand. A faint red nylon fiber flirts with the rug. I catch it later. For now I log the time in my head and reach for the guestbook to move it two inches away from contact zones.

Gran signs the witness line under her earlier entry to mark the liaison arrival. "Celeste Rourke present, 10:02 a.m., rules read aloud, no objects handled," she writes. She sets the pen down and fixes the tote with a glance. The volunteer smiles and offers a pin. Gran does not care about pins. She cares about the cat on the sign and the rule that protects it.

Celeste takes her mark beside the vitrine and the ledger, palms together as if she invented stewardship. She speaks a sentence about heritage. It would sell in a grant room. I let her finish the words, and when she lifts a hand toward the acrylic, I adjust the lamp. The light throws back her reflection and forces her to lower her wrist. She narrows her eyes, smiles wider, and closes with a line about our shared future.

The mail carrier claps once and then looks ashamed for clapping. He covers it by buying a paperback about maps and leaves a donation in the jar with a nod at Peppermint. Peppermint ignores the nod and collects a ribbon from the volunteer's tote with one sly paw. He bats it under the table and looks pleased with himself.

We restart the flow. Rafi filters bodies. Gran keeps the till in rhythm. I watch the vitrine, the ledger, the tote, and Celeste in a grid that has no corners empty.

A school group files in with a teacher who respects rope lines. They stand back and count spelling errors in the ledger. The teacher says, "People wrote the way they spoke." I like her.

At eleven, a donor with a tailored coat appears with two friends. Celeste brightens two stops and aims the donor at the stamp.

"Here is the original ex-libris," she says. "Our town's first mark." She touches the acrylic with two fingers. I wipe the spot the second she steps back and then look at her. She does not apologize. She considers and moves away.

I use a breath to look at the key in my pocket and check for weight. It sits where it should. I will not need it for anything except a demonstration later. Still, I check. The powder on the bow sheds the slightest memory into the fabric of my pocket. If someone does fish it out, I will read a line.

Rafi brings me a rag and points at the vitrine again. The hairline catches a new angle. I log the time. The scratch has not grown. It reads as a surface mark, not a gouge. It will help me later, not hurt me now.

We break for water. Gran rebooks a delivery that will now come tomorrow because I do not want pallets near the exhibit. She signs a quick note for the driver and tapes it to the back door. Her handwriting is the same as it was when she taught a room of fifth graders how to write checks.

The Chamber volunteer wanders to the map stand and strokes a print of the river with the pity of a person who wants to live in a brochure. She looks over her shoulder at Celeste and then back to the print. Her tote bumps the guestbook again. I slide the book two more inches to the right and set a book snake on its edge as a not-subtle barricade.

"Please keep bags away from the stand," I say.

She blushes, smiles, and moves the tote to the floor by her shoes. One enamel star pin catches the chain on the strap and twangs.

Celeste circles back to the table with her camera person, who I know from a short list of local videographers who work cheap. He sets a small tripod on the floor, frames the acrylic, and functions without ego. I like him. He is a tool, not a noise.

"Five minutes for a second pick-up," Celeste says. "Closer this time. No hands, your rules, my words."

I nod. "Your words," I say.

11

She gives the line again with an extra smile and a slower pause on the word original. The word is half right. The stamp was original when the first committee bought it. It is a set of stacked marks in a world where replicas exist. Words are as strong as the hands around them. I file that thought for later and keep my face kind.

The small team packs up. Donors peel away. The room returns to customers who want used paperbacks that smell like basements. We sell three, take in two boxes for trade, and write receipts in the neat ladder that makes my heart happy.

At noon I carry the key to the vitrine to the office for a double check. Peppermint follows me like a union rep. I set the key on the desk under the task lamp and turn the loupe to the bow. The dust sits in a light kiss across the grooves. I touch the tip of a clean cotton swab to the edge and pick up a trace. It reads gray on white. Good. Enough to transfer. Not enough to make a mess. I log the observation on the card taped under the table and give the time.

Rafi brings the spare micro fiber cloth and we clean around the base where tiny static catches lint. He grins when I hold the lamp to check his work. He likes when I check. It proves he is worth checking.

We open after lunch to a wave of townspeople who took an early break from desks and come with paper cups and questions. I direct cups to the cart near the fiction wall. I direct questions to the sign and to the index card of facts I wrote for staff so we do not invent on the fly. Peppermint patrols. He sits at a corner of the table and stares at the stamp head the way a cat stares at a bug in a jar.

At one, the Chamber sends a second volunteer to relieve the first. He wears a badge on a lanyard that matches the red nylon thread stuck to the edge of our rug now that the tote has made three passes. I use a lint roller and pick up the thread. I set it on a lab slip and note its color and time and position. He watches and opens his mouth to say joke words. He sees my face and closes it.

Celeste returns at two with a donor who controls a purse string for a project that will not help anyone who reads. I do my job anyway. I point at the ledger. I tell the truth. I do not sell anything a clerk cannot defend. The donor nods and calls the exhibit charming. The word sits on my tongue like sugar I did not order. I wash it with water. I do not grimace in public.

By three I have logged forty-two glances at the vitrine from people who ask permission with their eyes. I have cleaned eight breath marks, two fingerprints, one lipstick print that did not set and wiped easy with the cloth. The hairline scratch has not grown. The ledger under acrylic still looks like a promise. The stamp head under glass looks like a trap.

I take a photo of the table from above, a plain document shot with the binder card and the morning paper in frame again. I write the time on the counter card and sip water. Peppermint steals the elastic from my wrist and bites it once. I take it back and put it in my pocket with the key. His tail flicks. He forgives fast.

Gran runs the till with the rhythm of a dance she could teach backward. She takes a break long enough to walk the line that separates the exhibit from the rest of the floor. She checks the cones that keep the mop water memory in its lane. She writes a brief on the witness ledger, a one-line update for the hour. "Exhibit steady, 3:07 p.m., no handling, crowd light."

At four, Celeste reenters with a new plan. I can smell it before she speaks. She carries herself like a person who thinks she has found a workaround.

"Last segment," she says, smile fixed. "A donor wants a photograph of her hand in frame next to the stamp for scale. No touch. Her hand in frame, the stamp in glass, the ledger in range. No rules broken."

"Hand at four inches from the acrylic," I say. "Palm down. No rings near glass."

She wants to argue. She calculates. She settles. "Four inches," she says.

The donor has a manicure that costs more than my espresso machine. She holds her hand where I tell her and holds her breath as if oxygen will scratch. The camera clicks. I exhale when it ends. The donor thanks Celeste. She nods as if she saved the ship. She did not. I saved the glass.

As the sun reaches the front bay and throws late gold across the floor, the room softens. The tourist pair returns for a second look. The mail carrier peeks in on his way home. A man I recognize from city works stands long at the ledger and memorizes a name. His grandfather. He tells me so. He does not cry. He nods and leaves with a paperback of poems under his arm.

At five I switch the lamps to evening levels. Rafi sets the kettle for the last pot. Gran rests her pen and gives her hand a shake. Peppermint leaps to the sill and tracks a moth that will never make it through the glass. He is patient anyway.

I sweep the front bay. I pause at the hairline scratch and tilt the lamp to see it again. The line still reads front to back. No new arcs. No scuffs on the ledger float. The stamp sits fat and smug under its box. I feel the key in my pocket and touch it through the cloth for the hundredth time.

I set two chairs near the table for a brief talk at five-thirty. Nothing grand, twenty people, a simple laydown of what the objects are and why we asked them to sit here together. I queue a slide on the office monitor with three words and two dates. No clips. No music. No filler. Proof and restraint.

The small crowd collects. I speak from the left side of the table, away from glare and hairlines. I keep my hands open at my sides. Rafi resets a lamp with a finger. Gran stands at the back with the witness ledger open to a fresh line. Peppermint chooses the rug and closes his eyes.

"This is the Founder's Ledger," I say. "It records what people decided to fund when they had little. This is the ex-libris stamp they used to mark what they bought. We set them together today so you can see a decision and its mark breathe in the same room."

I talk for six minutes. No speeches. I answer three questions. Yes, the book is real. Yes, the stamp is iron. Yes, the Chamber brought it. No, you cannot touch. I watch Celeste in the corner of my eye. She smiles at the right times. She does not touch the acrylic. The camera glows. The donor in the expensive coat inclines her head and leaves with the air of someone who has done a useful thing by being seen.

We break up the small talk and reset the floor. Rafi flips the sign for the last hour to read Quiet Hour to help a man who asked for a place to sit with his grief in peace. The room obeys. The kettle sighs. The light warms.

Celeste waits until the last of the group fades and then steps to the table again. The volunteer with the tote edges close. The tote strap scrapes the guestbook stand. My teeth meet.

"Liora," Celeste says, voice soft now. "We need one clean shot of the stamp alone, no glass. It will take five seconds. I will lift the vitrine, not you, so your liability is zero. We will hold the base. We will not stamp. We only want a still of the mark face to face."

"No," I say.

Her smile fixes and cracks at the edges. "For optics," she says, like a child who thinks the right word is a key.

"No," I say. "For chain."

She looks at the key in my pocket as if she knows it is there. I do not touch it. I let the pocket hang calm.

"I am the liaison," she says. "I speak for the Chamber. The Chamber owns the stamp."

"You speak for the Chamber," I say. "You do not speak for the table. While the stamp sits under my roof, under my acrylic, beside my ledger, it stays in my custody. The rule is printed in four places. The witness ledger has two signatures under it. The camera saw the rule on your arrival. The key is not leaving my pocket."

Her gaze flicks to Rafi. He looks at her with the kindness of a person who cannot be pushed and smiles with half his mouth. She looks at Gran. Gran stares at the rules card and then at Celeste. The look is not unkind. It has no room for edit.

"Donors expect access," Celeste says.

"Donors get access," I say. "Eyes. Notes. Photos through glass. They do not get hands on the face. If you do not like how that reads, bring me a signed letter from the Chamber president. Tomorrow. With the date and the time and the phrase we accept full liability in nice ink."

The volunteer tries to rescue her with a joke. "We can draw a cat on a sticky note," she says.

"No," I say.

The crack in Celeste's smile becomes a line. She leans in, stops when her reflection fights her, and leans back. She considers a speech. She tests my face. She sees there is no sale.

"We will take the exhibit to the Chamber hall this evening," she says. "Safer there overnight."

"No," I say. "We close at six. We keep it under our acrylic and our camera all night. We break in the morning with the same sign. You may shift the exhibit when our witness and our clerk are there to log a transfer."

She opens her mouth. She closes it. She looks at the scratch on the glass and lifts her eyebrows, then drops them when I take a photo of the scratch again with the clock in frame.

"Half hour," I say. "You can have the last half hour with your camera, through the glass. After that, we cover the ledger with the curtain and put the vitrine to bed."

She breathes in, holds it, exhales. "Fine," she says. "We will do it your way."

"You always do," Gran says, so quiet only I hear. She writes a line in the witness ledger anyway. "Liaison asked to handle stamp for optics. Clerk refused. Rules restated. 5:42 p.m."

Rafi brings the microfiber and wipes a last breath from the vitrine. Peppermint jumps to the moderator's chair near the table and flops, chin on wood, eyes at half mast. He purrs once. Texture, not verdict.

The bell on the door rings. A neighbor sticks a hand in and waves without stepping over the line. The light outside has changed. Evening has opinions.

"Half hour," I say again.

Celeste nods without teeth. Her volunteer watches the tote and the guestbook as if they might decide to fight. The camera clicks and clicks. The stamp sits and says nothing. The ledger breathes.

I put my palm on the Founder's Table and feel the weight under it. Oak, iron, paper, glass, a town that wants the past and the present to shake hands and leave without broken fingers. I keep my hand there and count to eight for luck I do not believe in, and then I move my palm away.

The key rides the edge of my pocket like a fact. The barium dust waits to tell me if anyone stole a touch.

And for the first time all day I let the quiet sit, the kind that warns you how the next pages will read if someone tries to push past what we posted at the door.

CHAPTER 2

Window Hairline

The front bay takes morning light like a stage. By ten, it had warmed the rug, the plants, and the patience of the people who want a story to point at while they sip. The Founder's Table held steady. The ledger sat under its float. The stamp dozed under its acrylic like a stubborn king. Signs were posted where even the hurried could not claim surprise. No off-network devices near the exhibit. Hands off glass. No food. No moving the cradle. If you need a photo, shoot through my acrylic, not the air.

Peppermint sprawled on the register stool and watched the door. He lifts a paw when a group comes in, as if checking roll. Rafi tuned the lamps so glare lost its appetite. Gran held the counter with the witness ledger open and her pen ready to bite.

Late morning, the room reached that tight crowding that is not a rush and not a lull. People eddied around the Founder's Table. A stroller, two totes, three elbows, and one body that always thinks its coat is narrower than it is. The seam between order and accident narrowed.

It happened without sound first. A ripple moved through a body near the front bay, a bump at the edge of the display lane where we keep the map stand and the guestbook. A shoulder clipped the stand, the stand tapped the jamb, the jamb kissed the glass.

Then the pane spoke. Not loud. A crisp ping that felt like a fork on a thin plate. Heads turned. You could feel the inhale before the word crack found a mouth.

Mid-pane, a line bloomed like a pale vein. It started with a bright point the size of a lentil, then threw a single radial arm toward the upper left and a second toward the lower right. Two finer lines shadowed each, faint and curious. No shower of pieces. No rain on the rug. A live glass face that had changed its mind.

"Hold," I said. "Everyone pause where you are. Rafi, cones."

He moved before I finished. Gran's pen dropped to the counter. She did not say a word. She stepped to the front of the small crowd and set her palm out the way a person stops a dog at a curb. People obeyed her better than most signs.

I looked at the clock. Ten thirty-eight. I said it out loud and let it live in the air. "Time ten thirty-eight." I pointed at the body nearest the bay. A woman in a slate coat with a Chamber volunteer badge and a red lanyard strip peeking out from under the collar. Two feet to the left, a tourist with a camera that still wore its strap tight across a chest like a harness. A teenager with a tote from the thrift store had one elbow on the map stand. The map stand had moved half an inch toward the window. My eye measured these things whether I wanted to or not.

Rafi set cones in a half circle two feet from the pane. He wrote a quick card. Do not touch the glass. He taped it to the sill with that neat press he gives tape when he means it. He turned the lamps at the bay so they skimmed the pane. The crack caught light and told us its story line by line.

"Bodies within three feet," I said, steady. "Name yourself."

"Eugene," said the tourist. He looked stunned and sorry in equal measure.

"Tam," said the teen with the thrift tote.

"Paula," said the regular who runs the sign-up sheets for the block party.

The Chamber volunteer with the badge said, "I did not touch

anything." She said it fast. Fast belongs in a notebook.

Celeste stood a yard behind them in a narrow coat the color of dry wine. Her smile did not reach the eyes she kept on the pane. She lifted both hands as if to show she understood rules and then looked at me like a person who wants to cut rules into smaller rules.

"Everyone hold," I said again. "Nobody lean. Nobody breathes hopeful at this glass."

Peppermint rose to his feet and stared at the crack like a birdwatcher. He took a step closer, then stopped when he felt the cones had jurisdiction. He sat. He wrapped his tail around his feet. He blinked once. Texture only. He saves opinions for food.

I took the small pouch from the drawer and pulled a scale card, a loupe, a clean cotton swab, and the flashlight with the narrow beam. I set today's paper on the sill behind the cones where a camera would see it in frame. I walked to the pane with the calm pace you use when a room waits for you to set its heart back to rhythm.

"Gran," I said. "Witness."

She opened the ledger to a fresh line. She knows the difference between paperwork and witness work. This was both. She stood to my right with her pen ready.

I angled the flashlight along the glass until the crack lifted from clear to mineral. Spidering carries its own geometry. There are radial lines that shoot away from the impact, and there are concentric curves that loop around the origin. The side that got hit tells on itself. The crack edge will feel sharp on the side that took the blow. The back of the crack will feel soft. You can read it by touch without breaking it further if your hands remember how windows complain.

I took the clean swab and touched near the lentil-sized origin, barely there, far from the edges of the lines. The cotton kissed the surface. I slid it a hair along the main radial toward the upper left. The fibers caught. A small rasp. Sharp on this face. I tried the same test on the far side by opening the old transom two inches and reaching around with my other hand. The radial felt smooth there. I set the swab in a bag for no other reason than to keep minds honest.

"Impact reads from inside," I said. "Not thrown from the street."

The room exhaled like one body and then inhaled twice as fast. People love street villains. I love physics. The pane said someone or something inside started the crack. No rock from the curb. No neighbor with mischief. Pressure from our side. A bump, a hit, a kiss from a stand, a tote corner, a wrist with a ring. We would read the rest.

"Photograph," I said to Rafi.

He placed the scale card on the sill under the origin and took three shots. Full pane. Mid with horizon line. Close. Today's paper in the wide. Clock in the frame. He checked focus without commentary and sent the photos to the case folder labeled Exhibit Day.

I crouched and looked along the sill. Dust lives there like a quiet citizen. When it is disturbed, it reports. A thin bright line cut the dust where the map stand had inched toward the glass. Half an inch. The rubber foot left a scuff kiss on the painted wood. I took a photo. I put the scale card down and took another. I picked up a hair-thin red thread that had fallen from somewhere onto the sill when bodies shuffled. Nylon. Glossy. Dyed a clean red that clothes love to pretend is practical. I lifted it with tweezers, put it on a little glassine, and wrote the simplest line that did not accuse. Red nylon fiber recovered from sill, 10:41, front bay interior. I signed the slip. Gran wrote the time and the words front bay mid-pane crack reads inside-out in the witness ledger in the same hand I learned with.

"Do not sell a culprit," she said in a voice low enough that only I heard it.

"Not selling," I said. "Inventorying."

"Good," she said.

Celeste stepped forward, smile still on, voice pitched for calm leadership.

"Liora," she said, "for safety, we should move the exhibit now. The Chamber hall is two blocks away. Our cases are rated. We have museum gel and trained handlers. I can call a truck and a glazier. Donors need to see that we are decisive."

"No," I said. "We isolate the pane. We log the break. We put a temporary brace if I see change. We call our glazier who knows this frame and this age. We do not move objects while people's eyes are hot."

"Your glass could fall," she said.

"Could," I said. "Right now it reads stable. No ladder of crazing. Two radials, two mirrors, no open star. The frame holds. The weight sits right. We control both sides of the air. That buys time."

She glanced at the tote by the map stand, at the enamel pins that still clinked near the strap, and then at the pane again. She smoothed her coat. She used a tone people think sounds professional.

"We have an obligation," she said. "To the artifacts."

"I have an obligation to the chain," I said. "You can help by stepping back and letting me mark the zone."

Rafi had already unspooled the blue tape. He set a small cross over the origin to discourage wanderers from pressing their fingers on the lentil like a wish. He ran a U of tape around the lower half where a curious person might lean with a hip. He set a second card. Do not lean on the sill. The teen with the thrift tote backed up without me having to say a word.

"Bodies within three feet at the ping," I said, turning to the four nearest. "Eugene. Tam. Paula. And you." I looked at the volunteer with the Chamber badge. She tightened her mouth before she spoke.

"Marsi," she said.

"Thank you," I said. "Stay put while I log positions."

I took a chalk and traced the outside edges of their shoes where they stood, then numbered the spots on the rug. One, two, three, four. I sketched the map stand foot on a slip and measured the half inch we lost to the jostle. I put the tape measure from the sill to each chalk mark and read the numbers to Gran. She wrote them. I set the map stand back that half inch and took a photo of the scuff on the sill and the direction of the scuff, toward the pane.

"Who bumped," I said, neutral.

Eugene lifted a hand. "I think it was me," he said. "A shoulder to the stand. Not hard. Then that sound."

Tam pointed at his own tote. "I swung my bag when I turned," he said. "It tapped the stand. I did not think it was much."

Paula shook her head. "I was two feet back," she said. "Hands folded. You can write that. I did not touch."

Marsi said, fast again, "I did not touch anything."

"You are all fine," I said. "The pane tells me inside, and the stand tells me direction. The small scuff reads inward. We log it. No one is in trouble. We fix the zone and keep the day moving."

I looked at their hands. Tam's tote had a plastic clip at the shoulder, smooth. Eugene wore a watch with a rounded face and a soft band. Paula had nothing on her wrists. Marsi had a lanyard under her collar and a ring with a square stone that could chip a plate. The lanyard was red nylon. The same red as the thread on my glassine. I did not say the thought out loud. I wrote it later in the margin where it would be a note, not a verdict.

"Rafi," I said. "Glazier."

He already had the number. I heard him give the address, the age of the glass, the read on the break, and the phrase no emergency, but today would be generous. He thanked the voice and wrote a time. Two to four. Good enough.

Peppermint tested the cone line with one paw, then sat and

yawned. He blinked at the pane, blinked at me, and blinked at the volunteer tote. He has a talent for sitting near the thing that matters without telling me why. It is not help. It is a metronome.

We let the room loosen a little. People returned to the exhibit path, now a loop that gave the bay a wide berth. Rafi kept a shoulder near the cones. Gran posted a small note under the signs to explain the crack and soothe the curious. The note said what needed to be said. Mid-pane crack documented. Interior origin. Area stable. Please observe but do not approach. She signed her initials and stepped away.

Celeste waited until the room had redistributed itself before she tried again. She lowered her voice and stood where the camera on the ceiling could not see her mouth.

"This is a liability," she said.

"It is logged," I said. "You will get a copy of the report. You do not need to move anything."

"We do," she said. "If this cracks further tonight, you will blame the Chamber. If it does not and we fail to act, donors will ask why we stood there. Optics matter."

"Proof matters," I said. "If you try to move the case tonight, you will have to open my acrylic and take the stamp out of chain. We both know what that will look like on the page."

She smiled in a way that wanted me to feel small. It did not land. "We can write a receipt and have a witness."

"You will have my witness," I said, "and my refusal on the same line. You do not want that file."

She took half a step back and lifted her chin. "Then put it in writing that you assume full liability for the exhibit until the morning."

"I already have," I said. I pointed to the ledger and the note under the sign. "Signed. Time-stamped. You can photograph it."

She did not. She stared at the crack as if staring would make the lines change their minds. She waved Marsi away from the sill with two fingers, as if I had not already done the same with my cones.

Rafi called the time. "Glazier at two forty," he said.

"Good," I said.

We ran the day around the injury. Two school teachers came at lunch and brought their classes. We instructed in a voice that did not scare eight-year-olds. We showed them how to look without touching and how to read a room with their eyes. A small boy asked if the cat did the crack. Peppermint blinked as if offended. The class laughed and went away with receipts for two used chapter books and a lesson in not leaning on glass.

At one, the mail carrier returned with a sandwich and stood distance like a pro. He is good in rooms because rooms are his job. He watched the crack without staring and checked his watch at intervals in the way of someone who knows about schedules.

At one thirty, a donor with a loud scarf pressed her weight to the cones and I had to remind her that low plastic can hold a line better than her opinion. She smiled in a way that said she hated being told anything and backed up an inch. That inch is all I wanted.

At two, the glazier arrived with a small bag and a quiet voice. He nodded at me, nodded at Gran, nodded at Rafi, and squinted at the pane like it had scolded his child. He read the crack with two fingers and a small glass scraper he used like a stethoscope.

"Inside origin," he said, which is all a person wants in a partner. "No rattle. Your tap holds. I can put a brace strip on the face and a clip to take pressure off the top corner. That buys you your evening. It needs a full pane tomorrow. I will cut to fit at the shop tonight. Eight a.m. install if you like."

"Perfect," I said.

He set a thin clear strip over the origin and pressed with a tool that kissed the glass without insult. He set two narrow clips at the top where the frame had a bad habit of sagging after a season. He wrote a slip and I signed and Gran countersigned and

Rafi paid the deposit with a firm hand. The glazier left without extra words. He trusts us to call him back. We do.

The room relaxed when the clear strip covered the bright lentil. People like stickers. They think an adhesive is a charm. It is not. It is a brace. The pane held.

I checked the sill again for fresh debris. Near the right edge, where the brushwood plant shades morning light, a second red nylon hair had landed as if to make a point. It had curled around itself in a tight loop when static kissed it. I lifted it with a fresh tweezer tip and set it in a second glassine, wrote the time, and bagged it with the first. I did not look at Marsi's lanyard. I did not look at the tote strap. I looked at the floor, the stand, the chalk marks where shoes had stood, and the tape cross that now looked like a bandage.

"Log the names for the three-foot circle," Gran said.

I wrote them clean. Eugene, tourist. Tam, student. Paula, regular. Marsi, Chamber volunteer. I added Celeste, three feet eight, back of the knot, present at ten thirty-eight. I added that my swab felt sharp on interior face of radial near origin, smooth on exterior. I added the photo numbers. I am a boring person with a good binder. The city can thank me later.

At three, Celeste stopped her whisper campaign and raised her voice so the far corner would hear.

"We cannot host artifacts in a space with a compromised window," she said. "We will move the exhibit to the Chamber hall tonight for safekeeping and continuity."

Half the room looked at her. The other half looked at me.

"Correction," I said. "We will secure the pane. We will log the day. We will keep the exhibit under our acrylic and our camera overnight with a witness and a clerk. In the morning, when the window is whole, we will discuss transfer with the Chamber under signatures."

She smiled like a person who wants to call me stubborn and knows the word will cost her. "Stubborn is not a virtue," she said to her volunteer, which is how some people think they avoid owning a sentence.

"Chain is a virtue," I said, not to her, to the room. "Talk as long as you want. The rule does the work."

Rafi printed a small strip for the door. Window braced. Exhibit secure. Please keep distance. He taped it below the regular sign. The tape lined up, square. He loves lines more than he loves praise.

The light tilted and cut across the pane so the crack went quiet for a few minutes. You could almost forget it. Then the sun rolled and the lines flashed again like wire under frost. I took one more photo for the file and set the card next to it in the binder. I will not be told later that I let a line drift without record.

By four, the crowd felt less like a crowd and more like a set of people who had agreed to share a room. People count better when a thing has happened. They count their breaths. They count their steps. They count on me to count for them. I keep my end of that work.

The Chamber sent a second volunteer to relieve Marsi. The new one had a badge on a red cord and a tote without pins. He looked at the cones the way a person looks at a sign that warns of ice. He read the small card under the larger one. He nodded and took a position that did not flirt with lines. He smiled at people the way you do when you are being paid in soft power. He was not the problem, yet.

Celeste did not give up. At four thirty she made her appeal a third time, gentler, in a tone that belongs at a bedside.

"Let me get it done for you," she said. "I can have two handlers here by five. We can move the stamp under camera to a case that travels. You can sign a lovely chain receipt. I will bring a bottle of something to toast you when it sits in our hall."

"You will bring your bottle to your own event," I said. "My bottle stays corked until the pane is whole. Then we will talk about the next time we host this stamp. Not tonight."

She held my eyes for a beat and then looked away. The look was not defeat. It was a note. She would try again. She would find another door. She would call someone who likes phones.

Gran lifted the witness ledger and wrote another line. Liaison asked to move exhibit at four thirty, clerk refused, pane braced, crowd informed, glazier scheduled. She set the book down and stared at Celeste the way a person stares at the pencil that keeps breaking. The pencil got the point.

Peppermint found the last luck of sun on the rug and slid into it like a loaf. His ears tracked the door. His eyes stayed narrow. He sleeps through most trouble and sits up for the part that wants to make noise. I took comfort in the loaf.

At five, I walked the bay with the glazier's brace in mind. The clips held. The strip held. The crack had not grown. The map stand stayed where I set it, no one daring to breathe on it. I checked the sill for a third thread. None. Two was enough. I put the glassines in a sleeve with a label. Red nylon from sill, times 10:41 and 2:17. I set the sleeve next to the chalk mark sketch and the shoe distances and closed the binder on the page. The click felt right.

Two donors came to say goodbye to the cat. They told him he was handsome. He accepted the truth with silence. They read the window strip and nodded like grown-ups. They left their cups on the cart where cups go. The day breathed.

At five thirty, Celeste made her last play. She did not raise her voice this time. She let the word safety do it for her.

"Liora," she said, pulling her coat tight at the lapel as if the evening had grown colder, "safety dictates we move the exhibit to the Chamber hall tonight."

"No," I said. "Safety dictates we keep objects under known protections and a camera that never sleeps. You may stand here and watch me lock the case and watch me test the alarm and watch me sign the witness log with Gran. In the morning you will watch me open it again. That is the plan."

She held the smile. It looked tired. "Donors will expect action," she said.

"They are getting it," I said. "They are seeing a clerk who does not let noise move objects. If a donor wants to fund our panes so that I can let you wheel this table through town every time a line appears in glass, it will still be a no."

She lifted her hands an inch as if to wash them and then let them fall. She looked at the pane like it had insulted her. She looked at the stamp like it had robbed her. She looked at me like I was a lock without a key.

"We will be back at six," she said.

"You will find the door closed at six," I said. "We open at nine."

She turned to her volunteer. "We will reconvene at the hall," she said. "Prepare a statement."

He nodded with a face that promised things to the wrong audience. They left with a little rustle of lanyard and tote.

Rafi stood at my elbow the way he does when he thinks I might want tea, or a fight. "You will sleep," he said.

"I will sleep with the binder on my chest," I said.

"Romantic," he said, and went to the kettle.

Gran placed the witness ledger in front of me and tapped the line for my signature. I signed, time-stamped, and added the two words that had ended more fights than any speech. Pane braced.

The last customers paid for two paperbacks and stepped into the evening. Peppermint hopped off the stool and walked the cone line, sniffing once at the strip over the lentil. He sneezed and looked offended. He does not like adhesive. He likes his world dry and neat.

I turned the lamps to their night levels. I checked the vitrine, the ledger float, the key in my pocket, the tape on the bay, the chalk marks on the rug, the witness lines in the book. The room had taken a hit and not lost its shape.

I touched the pane, not at the crack, at the frame. Wood warm from the day. I closed my hand and looked at my watch.

"Time five fifty-six," I said for the ledger. "Front bay crack logged. Interior origin. Zone braced. Witness set. Exhibit remains."

Outside, the street took on the color it wears when signs change sides and people go home to say what the day made them think. The shop did not move. I did not move it. I raised the cones a hair so the mop tomorrow would not tangle them. I set the sign that says Quiet Hour back on its hook. I watched the door.

At six, I flipped the plate to Closed and locked the cylinder. Celeste's shadow crossed the window with purpose. Her knock arrived two seconds later. It was a polite knock. It wanted to be a key. It was neither.

I did not open.

She cupped her hands and peered in at the pane and then at me and then at the stamp. Her lips shaped the word safety again. Through glass, it looked smaller. She lifted her phone to her ear and turned away to make a call that would not move an acrylic lid.

Peppermint jumped to the sill beside the crack and sat with his nose an inch from the strip like a guard who does not care about titles. He closed his eyes. He slept.

I logged the minute in the witness ledger and put the book away.

Tomorrow would come with a glazier and a pane that fit the frame like a habit. Tonight the exhibit slept under my watch and the camera's red eye. The day had found its first accident and taught me what needed posting in bigger letters.

Celeste would try again. I could already hear her pitch.

Move the exhibit to the Chamber hall tonight.

No.

CHAPTER 3

Alley Body

Closing hours teach you which noises matter. The front window wore its brace strip. The cones kept visitors from leaning. The vitrine glowed like a calm tank. I had the key in my pocket, the witness ledger signed, the lockbox emptied and logged. Six o five. Gran flipped the plate to Closed and went to the office to total the till. Rafi rinsed the kettle, set the cone to dry, and checked the breaker for the night. Peppermint patrolled the rug's edge like a small marshal and then chose the register stool. Texture, not counsel.

I swept the path to the back hall and checked the exit light. The alley door sat in its frame the way it has for thirty years. Steel, stubborn hinges, keypad at eye level. I touched the handle to feel the day's heat and heard nothing but the kettle settling and the street's long breath outside.

At six nineteen, something hit wood in the back. Not a bar bang. Not a crate drag. The kind of contact that makes objects argue. One thud. One small scrape that followed it like a tail. Then nothing.

Rafi heard it too. We looked at each other and did not raise our eyebrows because we are not theater. He took three steps toward the hall. I took the same steps and stood in front of him.

"I go," I said.

"Copy," he said. His voice went flat and ready.

I crossed the hall, past the rare shelf where the old presses live when we remember we own them and want to look like adults. The air from the back was colder. The door to the alley stood half a finger ajar. The keypad glowed the way a screen glows after a touch. Peppermint followed me to the edge of the hall and stopped. He knows the rule about doors. He sat with both paws together and blinked.

I put my palm to the door, pushed an inch, and saw it. Body at the threshold, feet in, shoulders out, face turned toward the jamb, short hair caught on the rough steel plate. Celeste. No rise, no breath, no sound a room could save. A dark bloom at the hairline where iron does not forgive heads. Her blazer had ridden up and bunched at one shoulder. One hand still held her phone like a small promise. The other reached toward the shelf that holds our heavy cast-iron book press.

The press sat tilted on the edge of the high shelf above the cart rail, two feet in from the door. It had tipped like a lopsided moon off its base. One foot had kissed the floor. The other still rested on the shelf lip. The angle read swing, not drop. A line of dust on the shelf told an arc. I smelled citrus, fresh and clean where nothing else in this hall smells clean.

"Stop," I said, to myself and to anyone alive in the air.

I moved nothing. I put my shoulder to the door and blocked the jamb with my hip so a curious neighbor would not walk in on the wrong story. I did not kneel. I went to the wall phone. I called the number I know better than my own.

"Asa," I said when he answered.

"Say it," he said.

"Back door, threshold. Celeste on the sill, head wound, no signs of life. Cast-iron book press tipped from the high shelf near the jamb. One foot on the floor. One on the lip. I smell citrus wax. The keypad glows. The door was open when I got here."

"Time," he said.

"Six twenty-one," I said. I said it louder for the camera in the hall. "Time six twenty-one."

"Block the threshold," he said. "Do not move the press. Call it in and then read the room like a book."

He hung up without kindness. He does not sell it when you do not need it. I dialed dispatch and gave the script. Unresponsive adult, head injury, no pulse, scene secure, officer en route, medical en route, possible accident, possible tampering. I kept the words measured. I kept myself out of the scene. I hung up. I wrote a one-line note on the counter card. Found Celeste at back threshold, press tipped, time noted, calls placed.

Rafi slid to the hall and stayed at the line I drew with my body. He did not step around me. He looked over my shoulder with his eyes only. He could see what I saw and no more. He took two photos at chest height. Full frame. Then a closer frame with the phone still in her hand and the press foot near her shoulder.

"Peppermint," he said, without looking down.

Peppermint flicked his ear and stayed. He is nosy. He is not stupid.

Gran came to the hall with the witness ledger open. She stopped behind Rafi and did not ask for details. She read the look on my face, looked at the door, then put the book against the wall, used the top of it as a desk, and wrote the line that starts the next file. Six twenty-one, body at threshold, press askew, clerk present, witness present, staff present.

I studied the press. It is a heavy thing we inherited from the last people who loved paper. Cast iron of the old school. Two feet on the back, two feet on the front, a long arm that lowers a plate. We do not use it. We dust it. We say sentences about history beside it. Tonight it had decided to join the world.

Under the front left foot, on the concrete, a smear of gray with a shine. I bent at the waist, stayed away from the line that would make me part of the scene, and breathed. Citrus. Not old. The kind of scent that comes off the bottle when you pull a cloth and go after heel marks. Under the front right foot on the shelf, no smear, no shine. The foot itself had a clean ring where it had missed the floor. A mismatch. One foot knew our wax. The other had not met it. I put that thought on a card in my head and did not get cute with it.

At the base, a screw held the press to the shelf through a bracket. Four screws, one at each corner. Three wore the brown skin of years. One gleamed like a straight answer. Newer steel. Threads still crisp. Slot clean. No dust cookie around the head. Someone had turned that one recently. The bracket on that corner had shifted a breath compared to the other three. I took a long breath and did not say the words loosened and reset out loud. I would say them later if the metal and the holes agreed.

"Photograph the foot," I said.

Rafi passed me the scale card. I set it beside the smear without reaching into the line of dust that cracked near the press like a low tide. He took the shot and then a second of the opposite foot on the lip. He tilted the lamp so the citrus shine showed. He took a third of the screw heads. New steel, old steel. A person who loves pictures will see the arrangement and guess. I file it as evidence. I am a clerk, not a fan.

Outside, a voice called from the alley. "Liora," a neighbor said, not loud, not soft, "you okay in there."

"Stand back," I said. "We have a scene."

The alley lives between our wall and a title office with a ground floor camera. The neighbor who called runs a courier service out of a small bay next to theirs. He knows boxes. He does not make trouble. He understands cones and tape and the kind of voice I am using now.

"Do you need doors blocked," he said.

"Block your own," I said. "Do not let anyone stand on our sill."

"Copy," he said.

Asa's car reads like quiet. When it takes the corner at speed, it still elbows no one. He appeared in the back hall at six twenty-seven, mask on, gloves in his hand, eyes on the floor and then on the press and then on the door frame. He did not say hello. He did not ask me to move. He looked for breath. He found none. He put two fingers on the neck and did not find a pulse. He looked up past me and said, "Call the coroner."

Rafi had already made the second call. He holds time without making a poem of it.

"Time six twenty-eight," I said for the record.

"Say it again, louder," Asa said.

"Time six twenty-eight," I said, louder. I heard the camera in the hall click its own timestamp. It helps to feed hungry devices.

"Describe what you have," Asa said. He will ask me again under oath. He will ask me when I am tired, and when I am bored, and when a reporter tries to throw me off. Right now he wants the clean first read.

"Celeste at the threshold," I said. "Back and shoulders outside, feet inside. Head to jamb on right, hairline impact, blood pooled on sill and dripping to the step. Phone in right hand. Left hand extended toward the shelf with the press. Press is a cast-iron model, four feet, bracketed to the shelf base. It has swung off the rear feet toward the door. Front right foot sits on the lip. Front left foot met the floor. There is a gray smear under that left front foot that smells like citrus. The right front foot is clean. One screw at the front right bracket is bright steel and looks replaced. The other three are old. Door shows keypad active. I did not touch it. I blocked the jamb. The alley is quiet."

Asa nodded once, set his palm up for Rafi's scale card, and then put his hand down when he saw Rafi had his own. He looked at the screw heads and then turned his gaze to the track marks on the shelf near the base. A clean arc in the dust, the shape the press would draw if a person loosened two screws and let it pivot to the door. The old dust stayed behind the arc. The fresh dust existed ahead of it where the shelf had been clean enough to slide. Old and new. Mismatched.

He crouched, looked at the smear, looked at the clean foot, and then at me.

"Your floor wax," he said. "Citrus."

"In the front," I said. "We waxed the front window lane last night. Not this hall. If this foot picked up wax here, it came from a transfer. If it picked up wax there, it tracked in."

"You will prove it in the morning," he said. "Right now I want your nose on record."

"Citrus," I said. "Fresh. Not the bottled concentrate smell from the closet. Wiped this afternoon, the way our front lane still smells. Not faint. Present."

He looked at the keypad. The backlight still burned. Not for long. These things nap like toddlers.

"Rafi," he said. "Photograph the lock. Gran, read me the witness line with the arrival time."

Gran read her neat sentence. Asa let her finish and then asked the neighbor through the door for his name.

"Darren," the voice said. "Courier."

"What did you hear," Asa said.

"A thud," Darren said. "Before that a chime. Soft. Not your front bell, your back little ding that sounds like a new email. Then the hit."

I looked at Asa and he looked at me and neither of us nodded. We did not need to talk our thinking in front of the door.

"What time was the chime," Asa said.

"Six nineteen," Darren said. "I looked up because I had a box on my dolly and I always check the lane when I hear that sound so I do not clip anyone. I saw no one. Then the thud."

"You sure," Asa said.

"I run a courier," Darren said. "The chime in my head is stronger than coffee."

"Thank you," Asa said. "Stay there, please."

He returned his eyes to the press. The bright screw at the front right bracket sat in its hole with a slightly proud head. The slot had no burrs. Whoever set it had used a driver and not mangled the face. The other three bore scars. Old. Lazy. One had a crescent where a flat blade slipped once. Dust ring intact around their heads. The bright head sat on clean wood. New.

Asa leaned toward the bright screw and sniffed. Steel can carry the smell of fingers. He did not smile at his own work because he does not need to.

"Gloves," he said to Rafi.

Rafi handed them. Asa did not touch the screw. He pointed at it with a capped pen and said, "Photograph, three angles, and then one across the base to show relationship to the arc."

We built the shot list and checked it off. Rafi snapped, I read, Gran wrote. Peppermint blinked twice and stayed seated. He looked bored, which is what I want a cat to look like in a murder shop.

The medic arrives faster than television will ever admit. She stepped into the hall, read my face and Asa's, and set her kit down without urgency. She checked the obvious and shook her head at Asa. He nodded. She asked permission to cover the face and Asa gave it. She did her sad work with care.

Two uniforms took the alley ends and set tape. The tape rattled in a small wind like ribbon. People get nervous around tape. I watched the neighbor step back to his sill and lock his own door as if doors themselves could go looking for work.

I moved my body enough that I could see the rare shelf above the press. Dust. A finger drag path where someone had reached up higher than they should have earlier in the day to show a feature of a tool to a friend. Or to loosen a thing. The lip had a fresh scratch on the underside where the bright screw lives. A driver tip will sometimes bounce when it misses. The line matched the tip width of a small handle. I took a photo, then took a breath.

"Did you touch the press at all today," Asa said from the floor.

"No," I said. "I dusted the shelf edge at noon. I did not touch the base or the screws. No one with a reason should have. We do not use it. We show it."

"Who stood here after you closed the front," he said.

"No one with a key that belongs to them," I said. I held his gaze at the word belongs. He knows our codes. He knows who had them this week. He also knows who likes to watch doors for gaps.

He glanced at the keypad. The last digits told no story without the log. He would pull that from the lock's memory under a warrant. He would ask me to export the router's presence list. He would ask me to print the camera's motion markers. Right now he read the floor, the press, the back of a dead woman's head.

Gran stood with the witness ledger open and did not sit. Her hands do not shake at scenes. She rationed that skill years ago and gives me the benefit. She wrote an extra line where she thought my memory would thank her later. Chime at 6:19 per neighbor Darren, courier, title lane.

Asa stood. He planted his feet where mine had planted when I blocked the door. He looked at the phone in Celeste's hand. The screen had gone dark. He held out his palm and I handed him a paper bag. He covered her hand and then slid the phone inside with the grace of a person who cooks wrapped fish without breaking it. He sealed the bag. He wrote the time and the location. He handed it to a uniform who will put it in a box and write the same time and location again. The phone will tell him a few truths and twenty lies. We will sort them.

I checked the press base again without moving from my spot. The bright screw told me it had been out recently or replaced. The bracket under it had rubbed the wood, new scratches on top of old. Someone had given the press the kind of attention we give to objects we want to move without moving.

Asa took a small penlight and shone it across the floor where the smear lived. He tilted it until the shine went from flat to glitter. Citrus carries a pearl when it is fresh. He nodded at the light and then at me.

"You smell what I smell," he said.

"Citrus," I said. "From the front. Not from the hallway. We did not mop back here."

"We will carry that in the morning," he said. "Not tonight."

Two more steps lived between me and the press. I did not take them. I made a list instead.

One. Celeste had the kind of head wound you get from heavy iron with a momentum it should not have. Two. The press had swung, not dropped. Three. One foot wore the wax of our front floor and had touched concrete. The other foot had stayed on the lip and had not tasted wax. Four. One bright screw had taken the place of an old soldier. Five. The keypad had glowed as if a hand had woken it. Six. The door sat ajar in the way doors sit when a person did not pull them closed with care. Seven. A neighbor heard a soft chime at six nineteen.

I put the list in order of proof, not drama. I always do.

The coroner arrived with a small team and the quiet that follows people who work in final rooms. She looked at me with an expression that held the correct amount of sadness and the correct amount of distance. She took the measure she needed to take and then looked at Asa. He nodded. She looked at the press and then at me and lifted one eyebrow. I gave her the short version under my breath. She nodded again.

"Everyone out of the line," she said. "Give me the door."

I stepped back just enough to let her do the work, then stepped forward again to keep the jamb blocked when she moved away. Rafi adjusted the lamp for her. She thanked him without looking up. Gran wrote the time. Peppermint closed his eyes.

When she finished, Asa set his palm up for the small driver kit we keep near the cash safe for repairs. He did not open it. He set it on the cart where the camera could see him not open it. He looked at me. He did not have to ask me to speak the line that scolds the room when it wants to invent.

"We do not touch," I said. "We do not test. We document and we hold."

He returned his eyes to the press and then to the new screw. He pointed with his capped pen.

"File this under hardware for morning," he said. "Get me your last receipt for screws and a list of the last time anyone fixed anything on this shelf. Pull the inventory photos where the base shows. I want dates."

"Yes," I said.

He looked at the smear and then at the front lane in his head where the citrus has lived today. He drew an invisible line from the top of the press to the sill where Celeste's head met iron. He wrote in his notebook two words and a line that drew itself. Swing path.

I held my own pen and wrote the same words in my head. Swing path.

The alley gave us the usual chorus as the night slipped past six thirty. Distant voices. One cart wheel complaining. A gull that thinks every bin hides a meal. No more chimes.

Asa sealed the door with a strip and wrote the time across the tape with his black marker. He wrote it slow and neat, like a teacher who still believes in neat. He turned to the neighbor in the alley and said a thank you without the word. The neighbor waved one hand and went back inside to a life with boxes and clean conclusions.

"Gran," Asa said, "read back your last line."

She read it. Chime at six nineteen. I looked at the keypad again. The backlight had gone quiet. It would still report. Devices love to tell on themselves.

"We will pull the lock log," Asa said. "We will pull your camera motion. We will pull the router's presence. We will ask who kept a bright screw in a pocket."

He did not say that last part to me. He said it to the air. The air heard him.

I stood where I had stood since six twenty-one. My shadow kept the door from claiming anyone else. Peppermint gave one soft sound, not a call, an acknowledgment of evening. The room, front to back, felt like itself again. The exception stood on a cart with a strip over its mouth and a plaque in my head that read, in quiet letters, get the truth before this becomes a story someone else tells for you.

We let the coroner finish. We let the uniforms do the dull parts that save the case from clever hands. We let the alley breathe.

Asa closed his book. He looked at me. His face carried the same expression it always carries when proof begins to stack. Calm, not pleased. He does not do pleased at scenes.

"Lock the front," he said. "Keep the cat in. Keep the phone on. Sleep if you can. I will call when the lab says when."

"Copy," I said.

He paused at the door and added the one line that turns a night.

"Log the neighbor with the chime," he said. "I want his minute on paper."

"Done," I said.

We pulled back into the shop. Rafi set the stool where Peppermint could climb without jumping from a crime scene into a file. Gran closed the witness ledger on a line that read like a ledger should. Clean, dated, legible.

I looked at the press one last time before the coroner moved it to do her work. One foot kissed citrus. One foot did not. One screw was bright. Three were not. I do not draw conclusions to soothe myself. I draw them when metal and dust point the same way.

Behind me, the neighbor's voice drifted in from the alley, talking to the uniform who took his name. He said the sentence the chapter wanted.

"I heard a soft chime," he said. "Not glass. Then the thud."

CHAPTER 4

Guestbook Tells

A fter scenes break, paper starts. Bodies ask the room for silence. Paper answers.

The back hall held Asa, the coroner, two uniforms, and a press that would not stop being a press even when it behaved like a weapon. I left the jamb to them and returned to my counter. Rafi closed the staff gate and took the stool by the register. Gran set the witness ledger where we always set it when we must not trust our heads.

Front of house wore the brace on the bay, cones in a neat arc, signs up. The Founder's Table kept its calm. Peppermint tested a corner of the rug and approved with a blink. I breathed once, squared the counter mat, and brought the guestbook forward.

We treat this book like a neighbor. It sits where the light is kind, takes names without fuss, and tells us who cared enough to sign. I spun it so the last page faced me and kept my hands steady.

Rule one of a guestbook audit: count first, read later. People love names. Numbers tell you if the page carries more weight than the day can bear.

I ran my finger along the last two spreads. Twenty-six lines from morning through five. Six entries after five thirty. Three names I knew. Three I did not. Pen strokes tracked from neat to proud to hasty as people lost patience with their own script. I checked the time stamps. Folks add times when you give them a hint. Today's hint had worked. Most wrote a number on the hour or the half.

The two lines that pulled my eye wore a confidence that did not fit the end of a long day. Both said 6:05 p.m. Both sat four lines apart, as if distance would hide the twin. Both in Celeste's hand.

She has a way with a G that hooks low and kicks up. Her R starts with a tight loop, then flares. Her numbers lean to the right at the same angle each time because her wrist never learned to slow down. The two 6:05s carried the same tilt, the same pressure, the same little lift on the tail of the 5. The second did not look like a second. It looked like a copy made by the same hand in the same posture within a minute of the first.

I slid a thin sheet of acetate over the page and set the task lamp to a shallow rake. Pressure throws shadows. On both entries the downstrokes cut deeper than the rests. The pen had been the same or close. The angle screamed same seat, same reach, same person. I flipped the page, tilted the lamp again, and read the indents on the sheet under. Two grooves from the twin 6:05s pressed through to the next page. No grooves from the two names between them. Someone had added those two Celeste lines together in one sitting and then filled the space between with quieter hands later, or earlier names had left less dent.

Gran watched me work. She did not ask. She knows my face when the paper starts to sing.

"Read it back to me," she said, keeping her voice for the counter.

"Two entries in Celeste's hand at six oh five," I said. "Same tilt, same pressure. One four lines after the other. Indents line up on the page beneath."

"After she 'left' the room," Gran said.

"Yes," I said.

At five thirty she had made a show of being finished for the day. At six she had knocked on my window. At six nineteen a neighbor heard a soft chime in the hall. At six twenty-one I said time at the back door. This book sat here and took her pen at six oh five twice for a reason I did not yet need. I had the fact. That was enough.

I marked the margin with a pencil dot at the head of each Celeste line. I photographed the page wide with today's paper in frame. I photographed the two entries close with the scale card at the baseline. I shot the page beneath to catch the indents under raking light. Rafi brought the document arm and made a clean overhead scan for the file. Gran wrote a one-line note in the witness ledger. Guestbook audit, two entries in C. Rourke's hand at 6:05, same pen and pressure, logged.

I closed the guestbook to protect the page and went to the slips.

We run donations through two paths. Cash goes into the tin and gets a hand receipt. Card gifts go through the till and print from the small thermal beside it. Both leave trails. People trust jars and printers. I trust numbers.

I pulled the tin and the hand receipt pad. Gran had signed the top of each hand slip like she does when she builds the day. The pad showed five blanks torn since noon, all assigned names matched to a dollar. The carbon underneath told the same truth. Nothing funny there.

The thermal printer flickered with its little ready light. I tapped the feed for two inches of white to give a baseline, then opened the events pane on the front desk machine. Rafi had the PrintService Operational log up before I asked. He filters like a chef trims a steak.

"All donation slips since five," I said.

He scrolled. Five nineteen, Donation_Slip_173, one page. Five forty-eight, Donation_Slip_174, one page. Six twelve, Donation_Slip_174, one page. The six twelve line carried an extra flag in the event body. Reprint true.

"Show payload," I said.

He clicked into the XML. The grant of it read like a little confession. Document Name: Donation_Slip_174. Pages:

1. User: FrontDesk. Client Machine: Cat-Front. Submitted: 18:12:04. Printed: 18:12:05. Reprint: True. The spool path told me the same story in another dialect. \fp_render \Donation_Slip_174_reprint.ps.

"Print to paper," I said.

Rafi printed the event page and then the tiny summary table to keep nearby. He marked with a pen the three times and drew a line from the reprint flag to the six twelve entry. He used a shallow arrow that looked polite. He respects paper too much to stab it.

We went to the till tape. The cut had not run yet; Gran does that at end of day. I printed a short readout from the last hour. Five nineteen, donation twenty-five, tender card. Five forty-eight, donation fifty, tender cash. Six twelve, none. No tender. That gap is not a mistake. Reprints often do not touch money. They touch perceptions.

I opened the donation slip drawer and checked the stack. Slips 172 and 173 sat in sequence, carbon tucked behind each. Slip 174's carbon was here without its twin. The top copy had walked. That happens when a donor wants their paper to carry home. The reprint at six twelve suggested someone wanted a second top copy. Who hands, and why, belongs to a later page. My job now was to fixture the fact. Slip 174 printed once at five forty-eight and again at six twelve without new tender.

I wrote the three times on an index card and taped it above the printer. I snapped a photo of the printer queue with the time filter open. Rafi exported the PrintService log slice to a text file and dropped it into the case folder. He has a way of naming files that would satisfy an archivist. I let him have his joy.

"Celeste pocketed 174 at five forty-eight," he said.

"She put it in her blazer," I said. "I remember the motion. She wanted the name prominent in the pocket so the corner poked out."

"Who printed the six twelve reprint," he asked.

"We will ask the machine in the morning," I said. "It will tell us who touched it. Right now it tells us true at six twelve."

"After her second six oh five signature," he said, looking at the guestbook like it had taught us a trick.

"After," I said.

Gran stood between us with the witness ledger and read her line. Reprint flag at 6:12, slip 174, no new tender, clerk observed carbon present, top missing.

She tapped the counter with the back of her fingernails in a pattern that keeps my mind from running ahead. Four slow taps. Back to work.

I moved to the sponsor cards. We keep a stack of heavy cream stock for donors who like seeing their names near objects. They write their name, we post the card, they point at it while sipping. This town likes nameplates.

The stack sat in a small box by the guestbook stand. The top card had a neat blue line where a pen had gone off, then back on. The second and third were blank. The fourth carried a faint, almost imaginary circle with a shallow notch near the top. I lifted it to the light. It argued with me and then showed itself.

A ghost of an impression. Not ink. Pressure. As if a heavy flat face had pressed through another sheet and left its breath behind. The circle sat the right size for the ex-libris. The tiny notch at the top lived where our town cat's ear tips into the border.

I set the card under the task lamp and raked light across the surface. The circle rose. The notch sharpened. A tiny pitted constellation lived inside the ring, the kind that shows when metal meets fiber with grit in the mix. I did not say the word stamp out loud. I did not need to. The card said it without ink.

"Photograph," I said, and kept my voice from getting ahead of itself.

Rafi held the light at the shallow angle while I set the scale card with a pencil eraser. He took three frames. One wide with the box and the stack visible. One medium with the ring at center and today's paper in the lower left. One close to catch the pitting cluster.

I set the card on a clean sheet and drew a soft circle with a blunt graphite point where the pressure line tracked. I wrote the time on the edge. I put the card into a sleeve and labeled it. Sponsor card, pressure ghost of circle and notch, recovered from fourth position in stack, 7:03 p.m. I wrote no conclusion. I wrote no hope. I gave the object a name and a time.

Gran watched my hands and the angle of my lamp. She kept her face still. She does that when she wants me to keep mine still.

"Say the line," she said.

"A sponsor card shows a pressure ring where no ink lives," I said. "Circle fits the ex-libris. Notch sits where our cat's ear bites. Pitting suggests metal face."

"The stamp lived under your acrylic," she said. She pushed no opinion into the air. She wrote one sentence in the ledger. Pressure ghost on sponsor card, 7:03, photographed.

I went back through the stack to see if any other cards carried a mark. The fifth was clean. The sixth had the faintest crescent at the lower right edge as if someone had pressed from above while the stack sat askew. Not enough to call. Enough to make me keep my sleeves on.

Rafi pulled the security clips from an hour before. He likes to use the cameras without making the room feel watched. He scrubbed the front frame at five fifty to six fifteen and let me watch in the corner of the screen while my hands worked. You could see Celeste at five forty-eight leaning with her left hip at the counter while Gran wrote a receipt for a cash donor. Celeste accepted a card from her and tucked it into her blazer pocket with a motion that looked practiced. The guestbook sat where it always sits. No one touched it while she did her drama for safety.

At five fifty-nine, Celeste moved the guestbook two inches. She did it with the back of her hand as if she was straightening the line. She pressed the spine firm into the counter and slid it. The move made sense if you wanted to write, or if you wanted to use the spine as a thing to run something across. Her hand sat at the same height as a small brass key in another person's pocket that wore a dust that marks what it touches. I did not let that thought finish itself. Not yet. I made room for it later.

At six oh two, she wrote a name. At six oh five, she wrote her own name and time. She rose, smiled at nothing, turned to speak to her volunteer, and then returned to the book and wrote the second six oh five four lines down with the same tilt. She closed the book with her palm, patted the cover, and walked toward the back hall like a person who has found a new door to like.

At six twelve, the front desk camera caught no clerk at the register and no donor at the drawer. The printer blinked and fed a single slip. We will see a shoulder in the corner later when Rafi stabilizes the frame. Right now it told the simple truth. The machine did its work without a person at the till.

At six nineteen, the hall camera took a quiet frame and the neighbor heard a chime. At six twenty-one I said time at the door.

I stepped away from the screen, away from the ghost card, away from the guestbook, and into a room that had not been designed for this kind of night. Peppermint rolled to his side on the stool and yawned as if he had done all the work and handed it back to me.

Rafi printed the queue slice to paper and set it in a sleeve. He added a sticky for later. Cross-check with till rollback when we run the end-of-day. The sticky sat in a neat square and did not hide any ink. He takes pains with sticky notes. I love him for it.

Gran took the guestbook and placed a small strip of paper between the pages where the two six oh fives lived. She wrote a reference number on the strip and tucked a copy of that number into the witness ledger next to her line about the entries. She does this so the futures we do not control will be able to find the past I am trying to freeze.

I ran my hand along the counter where the guestbook had been, feeling for any grit that did not belong. The varnish told me the day's traffic with a fine sand I wiped into a tidy circle with a clean cloth. Near the guestbook's usual spot a faint, pale smear ran across the width of the counter like the ghost of a straight edge. Not sticky. Not wet. I set the lamp and raked the surface. Particles held in the smear caught light in a chalky way. I did not label it in my mouth. I photographed it for later and wrote a line on a small card. Pale line across counter at guestbook spine height, 7:12 p.m., photographed, no conclusion.

"Put the guestbook in the safe," Gran said.

"Yes," I said.

We bagged the pages that mattered in sleeves so we could show them without touching fresh. We boxed the book and placed it in the safe behind the file drawers. I logged the time and kept the key on me. This day had enough keys.

The room softened. The coroner's team finished in the back hall and asked Rafi for a copy of the camera clip from five forty to six twenty-five. He made it while I filed. Asa looked in at the counter and nodded at the guestbook box and the slip sleeves. He did not ask for my theories. He will later, in the way he likes to pull them like threads to see if they break. He only asked one question before he went back to the back.

"Anything that wants priority," he said.

"Two Celeste signatures at six oh five," I said. "A reprint for donation slip one seventy-four at six twelve without tender. And this." I lifted the sponsor card in its sleeve to the light. The circle rose. The notch marked a cat's ear. "Pressure ghost of a stamp on stock that should be blank."

"Photograph with pit detail," he said.

"Done," I said.

"Good," he said.

He left me with my binder, my cat, and a shop that still smelled a bit like citrus even though we had not waxed this hall.

I took one last pass through the slips. I counted the stack again the way I always do when I feel the day trying to slide out of my hand. The numbers matched. The carbon matched. The printer told one extra truth. The guestbook waited in the safe to back me up when someone tried to build a speech without lines. The sponsor card under light had a ring it should not have. The circle felt like a voice from a pocket I had refused to open.

I slid the sleeve with the ghost card into the binder, wrote the time on the counter card, and set the binder upright so the spine read what I had written on it last winter when we started doing this like a job that matters. First truth.

Peppermint hopped from the stool to the moderator's chair and tucked his paws under his chest. He watched me with one eye and the door with the other. He approved of the shelf where the press would not live tonight. He approved of cones and tape and signs that do not lie. He yawned at the card with the ring and dropped his head between his paws.

I looked at the circle one more time under the lamp. There are rings you toast with and rings you wear. This ring sits on paper because someone pressed metal where it did not belong. It will sit here until it lands where it belongs in the chain.

In the back, a stretcher wheel whispered on the smooth part of the hall. In the alley, the neighbor sent one last word through the tape to Rafi. "Heard the chime," he said. "Not glass."

I closed the binder and felt that small weight that comes when a piece arrives before you have the sentence to hold it. Good. Let it pressure the next hour into shape. I will name it when naming turns into proof.

The card stayed under the lamp. The ring stayed in the paper. The night held its breath on the other side of the door while Celeste's last minutes kept rewriting themselves in my head.

And the one thing she had wanted all day sat under acrylic,

untouched, while a ghost of its face lived on a sponsor card that should have been clean.

CHAPTER 5

Router Page

After paper, power. When a room lies, the network tells on it.

The back hallway hums in a way you do not hear until you aim your head at it. Router on the wall shelf. Bridge for the bulbs. Little UPS that clicks when the power flinches. The shelf lives above the file cabinet so casual hands do not reach it by accident or design. Rafi keeps a step stool near, tagged and logged like a piece of evidence, because he is not letting anyone pull a chair to touch what keeps our air clean.

He brings the stool. I bring the binder. Gran brings the witness ledger because she understands that you write when you are about to poke inside a box of numbers.

"Same drill as last quarter," Rafi says. "Guest SSID first, then leases, then association logs."

He opens his laptop, finds our admin page, and hands me the keyboard as if it were a ceremonial object. He knows I prefer to type the password so the room learns it is me. I key in the phrase slowly, because slow catches mistakes faster than speed. The dashboard opens. The graph of guests spools across the screen in a line that maps our day. There is a bump at ten. There is a slow shoulder from noon through four. There is a stretch of quiet around six with the kind of little spike that lives in reprints and empty printer hum and people who could not resist looking up our schedule while standing under the sign.

"Time," I say.

"Seven ten," Gran answers from the doorway. She writes it down. She uses the top of the file cabinet as a desk. Rafi lines his coffee cup lid up with the corner because he thinks straight cups help straight lines. Peppermint appears at my ankle as if routers release catnip. He does not climb the cabinet. He knows better. He watches the small green LEDs and purrs once, like a generator.

I click to the Guest network. Peppermint Cat Guest. Open with a splash page. Rate limited. Segregated from the register side. Rafi did that work during a winter when we fought a slow drip of spam and never let it back in. The client list shows three associations alive: my phone, Rafi's laptop with a guest token, and the camera that feeds my office screen. The rest of the day reads in the log below.

"Filter on five forty to seven ten," I say.

He sets the window. The page populates. Each association lives in a line with a time stamp, a device name if the device was chatty, a MAC address if it was not shy, a vendor inferred from the first three pairs of that address, an RSSI that tells you where in the room the handshake felt strongest, and a note that says where the client came from last. Some people do not like being watched. I do not watch them. I read the network that broadcasts its own story as loud as anyone will let it.

A line near the top catches my eye. 17:58:32 associate, client name CR-iPad, MAC D4:61:9D:XX:XX:XX, vendor Apple, RSSI minus fifty-four, SSID Peppermint Cat Guest, previous association unknown, DHCP lease granted 17:58:34. The log writes in twenty-four hour time because it does not want to translate for me. I translate for myself.

"Five fifty-eight," I say. "CR hyphen iPad."

Rafi tilts the screen so Gran sees the line from where she stands.

She reads out each field with the calm of a clerk writing labels for school supplies. She writes CR-iPad in the ledger and the time. She underlines the name once, small.

I scroll. The same device disassociates at 18:09:11. A clean leave. No deauth storm. No complaint. No ban from the bridge. The RSSI at leave time reads minus sixty-one, which puts the device further from the router than when it came in. The front bay sits at minus fifty-five to minus fifty from this shelf. The counter sits around minus fifty-two. The back hall drops to minus sixty. The alley sits at minus sixty-five and worse because brick eats signal.

I scroll again. A second association. 19:05:07 associate, client name CR-iPad, MAC D4:61:9D:XX:XX:XX, vendor Apple, RSSI minus sixty-two, SSID Peppermint Cat Guest, previous association Peppermint Cat Guest, DHCP lease granted 19:05:08. Either someone walked back into range or someone woke a sleeping device near my wall at seven oh five. We were closed. The coroner had left. Asa still worked the hall. We sat at the counter with the ghost card and the guestbook box. We had a device named CR-iPad asking for our Guest at seven oh five.

"Export," I say. "Associations and leases for that MAC."

Rafi clicks. He names the file with the MAC and the time window and saves it to the case folder. He is precise about cover sheets. I like that about him. He opens the DHCP table. The lease for that client shows an address we assigned at five fifty-eight and again at seven oh five. The lease offers carry the same client identifier each time. The router remembers this as a regular. The client remembered us too. The note field says cached captive portal accepted. Which means the user had already ticked our little square that says be kind, no nonsense, we log connections by MAC, not content. I wrote that sentence. It has saved me more pain than caffeine.

I scroll to the whitelist page. The list shows MACs allowed to reach our staff SSID and the Bridge. No surprises there. Then I open the remembered clients page. That list keeps the last sixty days of Guest devices, which helps when someone thinks they are a stranger in my house and my logs call them by name.

Halfway down the page lives an entry that does not belong to us. CR-iPad, D4:61:9D:XX:XX:XX, first seen 2024-11-18 during Chamber Silent Auction Night, last seen 2025-04-15 19:05:07. Rafi had tagged it last quarter with a note. Chamber pool device, labeled 03 during Poetry Night, allowed on Guest for donation kiosk.

Gran set the pen down, then picked it back up and underlined 03 with the steady hand of a person who enjoys confirmation at least as much as bakery bread.

"Same MAC," Rafi says. He drags the last quarter list from the folder. He still has the screenshot of the pool iPads the Chamber brought for a pop-up donation kiosk during a winter event when they did not bring their own hotspot. We wrote the MACs down and kept them because I do not trust people who roll carts into my shop and claim their gear is well behaved. CR-pool-01 through CR-pool-04. D4:61:9D:... for each, with the last pairs different. The one ending in the pattern where my eyes land now matches the one on our screen. Pool-03. Labeled CR-iPad by whatever hand holds it today. It was here at five fifty-eight. It spoke to us again at seven oh five.

"ARP table," I say. "RSSI map."

Rafi opens the tools page. Our little router is not fancy. It will still spit out a table of who it has heard and how loud. The seven oh five association carried minus sixty-two. From this shelf, minus sixty-two sits near the back hallway, not the front. That fits with doors shut, officers present, coroner gone, Asa's crew picking up strips of tape and labels with their quiet steps. A device near the back east wall would read around minus sixty to minus sixty-four. The alley just beyond drops to worse. Seven oh five says someone stood closer than the alley. Or someone held the tablet near the door while we worked the counter and the camera kept its red light on.

Gran writes those numbers because she knows the difference

55

between science and accusations. She writes "approximate position near back hallway" and "signal strength at associate minus sixty-two" in careful loops. Her notes will keep a lawyer from pretending we leaped.

"Who had Chamber tech in our shop after hours," Asa says from the hall. He did not wait for my end hook. He heard the question arrive from the numbers and gave it its mouth.

I keep my eyes on the screen. "CR-iPad," I say. "Pool device three from last quarter. Five fifty-eight and seven oh five. Guest SSID both times. Accepts our captive portal by cache."

"Who held it," he says.

"Not me," I say. "Gran will vouch. Rafi will vouch. The cat holds nothing without claws."

"Which Chamber hands were here after six," Asa says.

"Two volunteers left with Celeste at five fifty-four and five fifty-seven," I say. "Marsi lingered for two minutes by the map stand. A second volunteer arrived at four and left at five forty. Toby, the assistant, stopped at noon, then came back at five forty-five to bring pins to Celeste, then left at six oh two through the front. He could have stood by the back wall at seven oh five outside our notice. Or a device sat in a tote near the door and woke under a hand that did not know it was speaking."

I scroll one more time through the associations. The router keeps a record of unique device names if the devices behave. Many do not. This one did. CR-iPad. The name fits two explanations: Chamber Rourke, or Chamber Room. The pool list showed CR as the Chamber's prefix for Chamber Resource. The winter screenshot Rafi saved had the labels taped to the cases. Pool-01, Pool-02, Pool-03, Pool-04. The label CR-iPad on our log tonight tells me someone renamed the unit locally. A person who touches settings tends to be the person who uses a machine in meetings where they want to sound important. Celeste had that habit. Toby had fewer habits and more tasks.

Rafi brings up the association details. He traces the DHCP lease to a line on the switch. We only have two AP radios, one per band. The seven oh five handshake came on the two-point-four. That radio reaches further than five. That explains the minus sixty-two while in the hall. The device did not like the five gig because the wall ate too much. People love thinking they turn invisible when they step into a hallway. Radios disagree.

I export the full log of client names that touched our Guest from noon to now. Rafi saves the CSV to the folder, then prints a summary page with three lines highlighted. Five fifty-eight, CR-iPad associates. Six twelve, printer reprints slip one seventy-four. Seven oh five, CR-iPad associates again. He draws a thin pencil line between the first and second, then a thinner line between the second and third. He avoids arrows because arrows tell you who to blame. We are labeling a path, not a person.

"Write for me," Asa says, pen at the ready.

I dictate in short lines so Gran can echo without crowding the page.

"Guest SSID log shows CR-iPad associated at 5:58 p.m. RSSI minus fifty-four. Disassociated at 6:09 p.m. Reassociated at 7:05 p.m., RSSI minus sixty-two. MAC D4:61:9D:XX:XX:XX matches Chamber pool device labeled 03 during Poetry Night last quarter. First seen on our network 2024-11-18. Next seen 2025-04-15, 17:58 and 19:05. DHCP lease granted both times. Captive portal cache accepted."

Gran reads it back. I nod. Rafi hands Asa the printed summary. Asa studies the three highlights, taps the seven oh five line with the back of his pen, and looks past me to the back door as if it will answer for itself. It will not.

"Who had Chamber tech after hours," he says again. This time it is not a question. It is a hook he wants to hang the next hour on.

"We will ask the devices first," I say. "Then the people."

He almost smiles. It does not show. He puts the paper in his notebook under a clip and leaves us with our LEDs and our green blips and our cat, who is now transfixed by the port lights as if they are fish.

Rafi cracks his knuckles, which he only does when he is about to post a notice to our own system. He adds the CR-iPad MAC to a watch list. If it associates again while we sleep, the router will push a message to his phone and to mine. He restricts the device to Guest with no cross-lan. It already has no path across, but he likes belts and suspenders.

"Mac vendor says Apple," he says, as if we did not know. He looks up the OUI anyway because he enjoys the ritual. D4:61:9D belongs to Apple. Not that it matters. Many things belong to Apple. People treat those letters like proof. They are not. They are a stamp on a shell. We still walk the inner.

I look at the radio noise floor. The level sits normal for a night like this. No blasts. No storms. No flood of devices from a bus on Oak. The CR-iPad stood out because it writes its name and because we know its face. A hundred other MACs will pass by this week and never send a hello to Peppermint Cat Guest. This one thought we were still friends.

"Pull the remembered list as a PDF," I say. "Tag the four Chamber units from last quarter."

Rafi drags a rectangle around the entries and exports the page. He prints it, then circles each entry with a pen. He writes the first-seen dates next to the names because he hates flipping when a sheet can hold two truths side by side. He adds a post-it that says ask Chamber who held pool-03 tonight. He pins the sheet to the inside of the binder cover where my eye will hit it when I open to the case.

Gran looks at her watch and then writes a new line in the witness book. Router admin access 7:10 to 7:31, present LW, RM, GW. Associations exported. CR-iPad events noted. She places a small dot by the seven oh five time. She does this as a habit when she thinks a reader will skim later. The dot pulls the eye. She learned that as a teacher with students who needed help finding the right line. It works on police too.

I leave the admin page open to the associations list in case we need to point at it for an officer who wants to stand in my hallway and pretend that numbers are secrets. Rafi locks his screen, because he is not an idiot. He moves the step stool to the side and writes the time we touched the shelf on the little tag he keeps under it. He likes to leave trails for his future self.

Peppermint decides the LEDs have finished their show and retreats to the office doorway where he can watch both me and the back hall. He gives two slow blinks at the floor and flops to one side with his tail across his nose. Texture. He refuses to add analysis.

We walk back to the counter. Gran holds the ledger. I hold the binder. Rafi holds his cup and tips a drop of coffee into the sink, which he does when he knows his hands should not hold caffeine after a certain hour.

"Do not let the Chamber borrow our network again for pool devices," he says. He says it like a joke and not a rule. I log it as a rule anyway.

"We set that after Poetry Night," I say. "They can bring their own hotspot next time or write on paper like adults."

He chuckles and wipes the counter where a fingerprint thought it could linger. He does not speak, which is the same as agreeing.

At the counter, I tape the printed three-line summary above the printer next to the donation reprint note. Five fifty-eight, CR-iPad. Six twelve, reprint 174. Seven oh five, CR-iPad. Two short anchors on a little wall. The reprint sits between them like a pebble you find in your shoe after a short run. You did not think you needed to check your laces. You do now.

The front bell stays silent. The room keeps its night pace. The glazier plans his morning. The press waits for the lab to speak. The guestbook sleeps in the safe.

Asa steps out from the back, pulls the door to, and writes the time across the strip he added to the jamb. He sets the pen down on the counter and looks at the printed page with the three lines and the pencil connecting them.

"I want the Chamber's device list by noon," he says. "You will send the screenshot from last quarter. I will make the phone call to the person who acts like they do not have time for calls."

"Yes," I say.

"Who had Chamber tech in our shop after hours," he says a third time, and this time it sits like a question set in the middle of a test.

"Your question has a MAC," I say. "It will have a hand tomorrow."

He nods without showing pleasure and leaves me with the quiet point at the end of a chapter that has run its pace. He walks back down the hall toward a door strip and a press and a corner of concrete that smells like citrus more than it should. He keeps his book open. He always does.

I sit with the binder and write a card for the file so no one will miss the weight of the network we pulled. I write it in the same blunt style I use when I want the line to outlive whatever drama arrives on top of it.

Router ties a Chamber pool iPad to Peppermint Cat Guest at 5:58 p.m. and again at 7:05 p.m. MAC matches last quarter's pool-03. Guest only, captive portal cached. Signal at 7:05 suggests back hallway, not street. Device does not belong to us.

I slide the card into the binder, press the clip, and breathe in the smell of paper that has already done good work. Peppermint snores. Rafi thumbs a label roll and writes CR-pool-03 on a little slip that will stick inside the folder when my head is elsewhere tomorrow. Gran closes the witness ledger and lays her palm on it for one second like a person who knows what counts in a shop like ours.

When we close for real, I will take one last pass through the admin page. If the line lights at two in the morning, I will wake. If it does not, the question will sit in Asa's book until he writes an answer that belongs to a hand. Tonight is numbers. Tomorrow is people.

I look at the clock. Seven thirty-two. The sheet with the three lines brightens under the lamp for one blink when I pass by, as if the printer wants credit. It does not get it. Proof owns the line. People answer to it.

We keep the lights steady. We keep the door shut. We keep the router honest. And in the back of my head the words repeat, not from worry, from rhythm.

Who had Chamber tech in our shop after hours.

CHAPTER 6

Press Feet

Morning gives you light and enough quiet to hear what metal says. I took it.

We opened late. The bay pane wore its brace. The tape line kept bodies two feet off the glass. The Founder's Table sat like a judge. The back hall smelled like paper and a faint hint of cleaners left by the coroner's team. No citrus here. Good. That belongs where I put it, not where someone wants me to think it went.

Rafi rolled the tool cart to the rare nook. The press waited on its high shelf, reset to neutral with two supports under the plate so no one takes a surprise. Asa gave me a nod that stood in for five sentences. Read it. Do not guess.

The supplies shelf sits five feet away. Two rows of bottles, a crate of felt sliders, a crate of peel-and-stick floor pads, rolls of blue tape, spare gloves, a box of cotton swabs, a small notebook where Rafi logs what leaves that shelf and when. I like that book more than I like most apps. It never crashes. It can be read during a blackout.

"Yesterday," I said.

Rafi opened the small notebook and read my line from last night. Front bay lane waxed, 7:14 p.m., product Citrus Clear Floor Wax, batch CC-31, two pads used, one cloth. He wrote the time off the register, then circled the words bay lane. We did not touch the back hall. I wanted that in ink in a place I do not carry in my head.

I pulled the CC-31 bottle from the shelf. The white cap held a drip that dried to a thin gray shine. Citrus oil with a silica carrier does that in our light. I opened the cap and let the air in the bottle touch my nose. Orange peel, not fake candy, with that tiny glue smell you get when polymers dry. I closed it and wrote the batch on an index card. You do not need a lab if you pay attention when you buy supplies.

"Pads," I said.

Rafi lifted the fresh pack we cracked last night. Eight peel pads in a sheet when it left the case. Seven left in the sheet now. He slid the cardboard sleeve from the trash and checked the till for the receipt. He had paid at 10:11 a.m. yesterday when the hardware store opened. He printed the receipt for the file. Seven left means one pad went somewhere after we finished the bay. We used two cloth pads on a block last night, not peel stick. Peel pads live under ladder feet and heavy things when you want to quiet a drag. We logged none of that.

He held the peel-pad sheet up so the holes where pads were removed looked like small moons. One hole. Position top right.

"Count your pads," Gran would say. She has said it since the year I was twelve and thought missing anything by one did not matter.

I wore nitriles. I carry a box of size small in a drawer that makes me happy every time it slides easy. I took two clean cotton swabs and the scale card and the task lamp. Rafi placed a clean mat on the cart and rolled it under the press shelf. The press showed us its four feet like a stubborn mule. Back feet ringed with dust cookies that take a season to form. Front right foot clean. Front left with a gray bloom at the heel that matched the smear on the concrete from last night. The room still held a faint citrus that did not belong to this hallway. It was quieter now. Present enough to argue. Not enough to intoxicate.

"I am going to touch nothing," I said to the room, to Asa in the hall, to our own camera above the fire door. "I will sample from the smear on the floor, sample from each front foot, then sample from the bottle to compare scent and shine. After that I will run my poor-person's match. If the lifts behave, we call the lab for an FTIR tomorrow to make a pretty print for court. Today we need a reasonable link."

Asa said nothing. He does not supervise with words when I write my own recipe on the fly and follow it like a clerk.

I swabbed the concrete where last night's gray patch had dried. I did not grind. I lifted and rolled so the cotton kept what it found. The swab head picked up a fine film with a faint sparkle where silica likes to flash. I bagged the swab and wrote the place and time and position. Front left foot smear, concrete, 08:37. I took a second swab and touched the clean front right foot for a control. The cotton came up dull with plain dust. I bagged it. I took a third swab to the front left foot where the bloom sat on iron. The cotton drank a thin stripe of gray with a scent that climbed fast. Citrus. I bagged it and wrote the line.

Rafi held the lamp at a shallow rake. The gray on the foot read as a skin over pitted iron. Under the skin you could see the little moons that cast iron holds when someone pours it in a hurry. The gray film rode those pits like water on cobble. The other foot had nothing like it.

"Bottle," I said.

I touched a fresh swab to a small well I poured on the cap. I dragged the swab across deglossed iron at the very edge of the base where our lift would not matter. The swab took up a wet line and then a dull line as the solvent flashed. I set that swab on the mat.

The test is simple and mean. Citrus wax under cheap UV kicks a shy green in our room. It is not a miracle. It is a blend of the oil and the silica, and it hates some plastics. It loves paper and iron.

The bottle brand lives in a weird middle ground. It likes to glow under our small wand. Other brands carry no glow or kick a blue that says more polymer than orange. I run this on the regular because I use what I can afford and my brain loves dumb light.

Rafi killed the front lamps near the nook. We let the bay keep its brace and its ambient. I turned on the tiny UV wand that looks like a toy and passes for a field kit when you need a direction.

The bottle swab glowed a narrow green across its wet half and then turned weak as the carrier dried. The lift from the foot of the press glowed the same green at the same strength and then faded at the same pace. The smear-lift from the floor kicked the same green and died at the same speed. The control from the other foot did nothing. No glow. No hint. Dead cotton.

Asa stepped two feet closer when he saw the three little lights answer each other like cousins. He did not sigh. He does not do poetry at scenes.

"Say it clean," he said.

"Yesterday we waxed the front bay lane with this bottle," I said. "This morning the left front press foot wears that wax. The floor smear under that foot wears it too. The right front foot is clean. The match on glow and fade argues same product. Fresh enough to glow. Not a ghost from past seasons."

"Not this hall," he said.

"Not this hall," I said. "We did not wax here. It must have traveled on a foot from where we worked, or the foot kissed a surface that held it. The smell says carry from the front. The glow strength says less than day-old. If it were from a week ago, the scent would be gone and the glow would be nothing."

Gran wrote exactly that. She did not improve my sentences. She let my clunky clerk words live. Good. I write for lawyers as much as lovers of stories.

"Transfer test," I said.

Rafi raised an eyebrow because he knows where I am going. We keep glossy test cards on the shelf for bookplate work. They take wax the way a lesson takes chalk. I laid three down and wrote bottle on one, foot on two, floor on three. I touched the bottle to card one, the foot bloom to card two, and the floor smear scrap to card three. I passed the wand at them and counted under my breath. I wrote the fade times on the cards. Forty seconds before the green sank below what my eye likes to call signal. Forty-one for the foot. Forty-two for the floor. No lab would hang a verdict on a second. A clerk can build a ladder with three rungs this close.

Rafi took photos of the cards under UV and then under room light and wrote the times next to each. We slid them into sleeves. I tucked the sleeves behind a tab in the binder I labeled Floors last winter for a different case in a different hallway. I love ugly tabs that make sense.

"Pad," I said.

He lifted the peel-pad sheet again. The missing circle at the top right would match a foot this size if someone had wanted to stick cushion under it and stop a squeak or hide a skid. The sheet glue catches dust around empty spots differently from the spots that still hold pads. You can tell how long a pad has been missing by how the exposed glue skin dulls. This missing one read recent. The glue at the empty cut sat clear, not film-gray. If the pad left yesterday afternoon or this morning, that is how it should look.

"When did you open this package," I asked.

"After coffee," Rafi said. "I stocked the shelf at ten twelve with the order from the hardware run. I cut the sleeve, counted all eight on the sheet, slid the sheet inside the crate. I never took one off. We did not touch peel pads last night."

"Log it," I said.

He wrote a small line in his supply notebook with the time. Gran copied it into the witness ledger because she hates losing details when we all get tired.

I set the peel-pad sheet beside the press, not close enough to touch iron, close enough my eye could compare sizes without lying to me. It looked right. Close is not enough for proof. I do not lie to myself to feel smarter. I filed it under watch this and moved on.

Rafi opened the drawer under the shelf and handed me a loupe. I tilted the press foot and looked at the bloom edges. No consistent fibers. A few grit motes, pale, the kind the wax carries. Nothing that screamed felt. If a pad had been on there this morning and then traveled, I might expect fiber husks in the wax skin. The bloom looked clean. That can still mean a pad left and took its fibers with it. That can also mean no pad. The missing pad from the sheet belongs to someone. It may not belong to the press.

I looked at the shelf lip. The underside where the bright screw lives had a small fresh nick that still showed bright wood, not oxidized. Asa had seen that last night and voiced nothing until he had enough to fill a sentence with spine. The top edge of the shelf wore a smooth arc where dust had been swept in a curve by something heavy. It started three inches left of where the press sits in neutral and ended at the edge nearest the door. The arc matched what a swing does when a press pivots toward a head at the jamb.

Peppermint leapt to the rare shelf below and sat, eyes on the top. He does not like shelves that watch him. He blinked at the top and then at me and then back at the top. His tail swished once. I looked where his eyes returned.

A dust swipe I had not seen in last night's light arced across the top board where we used to display a small platen, long ago. A finger or a cloth had cut a clean smile through an even layer of gray. Not new from this morning. Recent enough to read white against gray. It matched the path where a hand would reach to steady metal and then pull it an inch, then an inch more, then settle like they had rehearsed. Not proof. A track. I held it and did not point yet.

"Plaster lift from the concrete," Asa said.

I took one tape lift from the gray smear zone on the floor and stuck it onto a glass slide so the lab can pick silica under a proper light later. I am not addicted to toys. I know where fancy beats clerk hands. We will hand the lab the bottle, the slides, and ask them to speak for us in full sentences.

"Now the transfer proof," I said. "We make our own scrape and see how it behaves."

I walked to the front bay lane where we waxed last night. I chose a corner near the book cart where I would not ruin anyone's day with a dull patch. I cleaned a two-inch square with water and let it dry under the fan while I set up. Then I laid a thin coat of CC-31 with a clean cloth block and let it flash to that good satin. I lifted the floor number plate from under the cart wheel so it would not stamp a second vocabulary into my square.

Rafi brought the old cast-iron doorstop from the office. It weighs near the same as one press foot and has a base that reads iron the way the foot does. He cleaned it with a rag until no dust caught under the loupe. He set it next to my wax square.

"A tap," I said, "with the weight we think the foot carried."

He held the doorstop upright and set one corner down on the square, then rolled it forward to mimic a foot meeting wax during a pivot. He lifted it and I bent close. Gray bloom on the iron edge where the oil met pits and laid down. The bloom looked like the one on the press foot. I touched it with a swab, sniffed, and caught the same string of orange. I hit the wand. Green again, forty seconds to fade. I bagged the swab and labeled it for control. The floor patch held a smear like the concrete patch in back, scaled to gloss and not rough. I hit that with the wand. Same green, same fade. Rafi took photos of the new square, urine-yellow under UV, then the normal glossy after.

Asa watched with no expression. He likes this kind of grammar. A simple act, a simple echo.

"Say it," he said again.

"A press foot picked up wax from the front lane last night and transferred it to the rear foot and to the concrete when it swung toward the door," I said. "The other foot stayed clean on the lip. Our control performed like the scene. Product, scent, glow, fade, transfer. Fresh and local."

"Fresh and local," Gran repeated as she wrote. The phrase tasted like a diner special when she said it. It will sound like a hammer when we read it to someone with a lawyer.

I checked the felt slider crate anyway and counted. Twelve small felt sliders last week. Twelve today. So no one slapped a felt foot under the press and called it good. I checked the peel-pad case a second time. Seven in the sheet still. The missing pad had not fallen free in our own crate. I looked under the cart wheels for a peeled circle. Nothing.

"Pad goes in the file as a seed," I said to Rafi. "Do not marry it yet."

"I do not marry anyone," he said. He smirked and set the sheet back with the glue side covered. He slid the supply notebook behind it like a backstop.

We moved back to the high shelf. I brought my light up and set it to rake. The top board shows everything if you ask it in the right light. The dust swipe I clocked when Peppermint stared took shape. It formed an arc like the cut the press base would trace if a hand steadied the top while the base pivoted. The arc started at the old home position and curved toward the door hazard. The swath had that finger-width feel in the edges. You do not make that with a sleeve unless you rub. You make it with palm and three fingers when you lean and then pull. I took a photo with the scale and wrote the time. I did not include the cat in the frame. He is a diva and should not be a reference point.

Asa put one finger under the shelf edge where the bright screw sits. He did not touch the screw. He looked at the nick near the hole that read driver slip. He did not shift his weight. He took the photo I had asked Rafi to take last night again, at the same angle, so the lab can count the wood fibers that show fresh cut. Two photos taken by two hands in the same light will save an argument later about staged drama.

I looked at the bracket itself. The paint on it had a tiny crescent of shine where a washer has turned within the last day. You can read washers in gloss. A matte ring forms, then a bright bite at a new stop. The back brackets did not show that shine. The bright screw bracket did. I took a macro with our little lens. Nothing fancy. Honest pixels.

I stepped back and rolled my shoulders. My hand wanted to write a block of names and leads on the counter card. I told it no. Not yet. We need body, not gossip.

We wrapped the small test cards. We labeled the swabs. We cleaned the wand. We set the bottle back on the shelf and put a small red dot on the cap so a person with a badge knows which one we used when they ask and opens the right cap to sniff.

Asa picked up the pad sheet and took a photo of the missing spot with the batch number on the sleeve. He placed it where he found it because he respects my shelf the way I respect his scene lines. He looked at me and at the binder and at the press.

"You give me a ladder," he said. "I will climb it later."

"You will climb with a warrant and a sober smile," I said.

"That is the only kind of smile I own," he said.

Rafi laughed once, short. He carried the tool cart back to the counter and wrote the wipe log for the UV wand because he does not want us to leave our own residue and tell on ourselves later. He writes that like a priest at a font. It keeps him honest.

I put a sticky in the binder on the pad page. Hardware run receipt at 10:11, peel pad sheet missing one circle, glue edge clean. I will find that circle before chapter ten or it will find me when I do not want it. Either way, the empty hole here is a clock. That is what clues are when you stop fussing with them. Timers you cannot see until they ring.

The bay held. The cones did their quiet job. The brace strip lived like a thin bandage. The brace glazier would be here any minute to cut out the old pane. I looked at my watch and wrote a line in the counter card about the window so I would not forget the visit. Schedules have teeth. They bite people who do not respect them.

"Back to the scene," Asa said. He wants the back door before lunch to be a chamber where he can hear echoes off truth, not off voices. We gave him space.

I stayed in the rare nook a minute more. Peppermint jumped up one shelf, then another, and sat level with the top board where the dust curve lived. He did not touch the board. He put his nose a whisker away and breathed. Then he blinked in a slow pattern that I have chosen to believe means I have his attention, not his approval. Cats do not approve. They accept.

I stepped onto the step stool and followed his eyes. The arc caught a ray from the front that made it look like a river. It ran from neutral to the door edge. Right where the center of gravity shifts. Right where a person either stops because they value heads or pushes because they fear being seen with proof.

I took the last photo and tucked the stool back beside the supplies shelf. Rafi will write the time the stool moved on his little tag. He will feel satisfied. I will feel safe. Asa will feel ready.

Gran brought me the witness ledger so I could sign the test summary in my hand. I do not let anyone else own my lines. I wrote fresh and local one more time and underlined it once. I stopped myself from writing it twice. Once is how far truth goes in this room. Twice starts to look like sales.

"Coffee," Rafi said.

"Yes," I said.

He poured. I blew across the top of the mug and watched the ripples fix themselves. Peppermint snuffed a dust mote and sat like an idol. Somewhere outside a truck braked and a bicycle bell rang. Inside we held still while the building spoke through its floor. It does that when weight changes. You learn to hear it if you live with shelves.

Asa's voice from the hall reached us without force. "We pull the lock log and the router clip at noon," he said. "Then I call the Chamber and ask who held pool-03 after hours."

"Ask them about peel pads too," I said.

He did not answer. He does not encourage my hobby of throwing bones before he asks for them. He will eat the one he wants when the time comes.

Peppermint kept staring at the top board. He blinked and then held his eyes half closed the way he does when a sunbeam hits the right place. I resisted the urge to tell him good job. He would only pretend to ignore me, and then preen. I let him own the silence.

I stood in the rare nook and felt the day lean toward me. We had a bottle and a glow and a smear. We had a foot that wore the front lane. We had a second foot clean, which means the swing did what a swing does. We had a missing peel pad that would land where it lands when it decides I deserve a little gift. We had a dust arc on the shelf where a hand steadied iron and then let it go toward a door that was not ready for metal.

Fresh and local. Say it until you can smell the orange in your sleep.

Peppermint blinked again at the top shelf and then looked right into my eyes, slow. I looked back. We both knew what he wanted me to write.

I wrote it.

Fresh dust swipe arcs where the press sat.

CHAPTER 7

Stamp Bite

We closed the office door and set the task lamp to a tight cone. No guests. No phones. Chain first.

The acrylic still covered the stamp on the Founder's Table. I did not lift it alone. I asked Asa to stand in the doorway where the hall camera could see him. Gran held the witness ledger and the small clock. Rafi framed the office camera on the desk so the lens would catch every hand and every object. Peppermint watched from the file cabinet like a furred gargoyle, tail over paws, no opinion offered.

"Read the line," Asa said.

Gran wrote it and read it. "Vitrine opened for controlled test. Clerk L. Wren removes stamp head to office under witness at 8:42 a.m. Hands gloved. No ink used. Purpose: compare bite against registry card."

I took the key from my pocket. The barium dust still kissed the bow. I held it in view of both cameras, unlocked the vitrine, and left the base on the table. I cradled the iron head on a folded towel and carried it to the office. Gran wrote the transfer time and watched the door close. Rafi set the task lamp to the height I like for metal. Asa stood where he could stop me from making a mistake and also stop anyone else. We do not add drama. We put gravity in the room and let it do what it does.

I set the stamp head on the felt mat beneath the lamp. The face looked the way people want it to look. Round border, the town cat in profile, text that claims the library. Honest weight. Enough age to take a nice photo. People stop there and call it good. I do not stop there.

"Registry card," I said.

Gran took a smaller box from the safe and opened it like a jewelry case. Inside sat a cream card in a sleeve with three tiny punch marks that show it is not a prop. The card holds the authentic impression we use as standard. Gran's initials live in the corner. The year sits under them. The card shows the bite of the original die from the day it returned from restoration, ten years back, when she and the old foreman pressed one test together and photographed it for the file.

I placed the card to the left of the lamp, stamp head to the right, a clean scrap in between. I did not dip ink. I do not need it for bite. Paper tells the difference without color when the die meets it with pressure and the right support. I slid a piece of thin foam under the scrap to give the face something to sink into. I put on fresh nitriles. I let my hands go slow.

"One test," Asa said.

"One," I said.

I set the stamp face down on the scrap, no twisting, no show. I pressed with a flat palm and counted five, the cadence I use for bookplate proofs, the count that keeps hands from rocking. I lifted the head and set it aside. The impression rose without ink. You could see the ridge where fiber shifted, the tiny valleys where the metal's pits had pressed air into paper. Not a bold image, not a silence either.

I slid the scrap under the loupe. The bite around the outer ring looked a hair soft at two o'clock, a little loud at eight. The cat's ear showed a clean tip without a notch. The letters had a bass I did not expect in the lower curve, as if the rim there sat proud. I tilted the lamp and let the relief throw a shadow.

"Half a hair off," I said. "Outer ring sits wider at eight than it does on the registry. The bite at two is shy where the card shows an even press. If I overlay, the difference runs the width of a fine pencil line."

"Show your overlay," Asa said.

I pulled the acetate overlay from the folder. Last year I traced the registry card's ring with a 2H pencil and punched three registration holes to anchor future tests. I dropped the sheet onto the scrap so the anchor holes met the pins on the tray. The overlay ring floated a breath outside the fresh impression from ten to two, then fell inside it from four to eight. The shift was small, half a hair, but consistent. The ear on the overlay showed a minute flat at the tip. The ear on the fresh bite came to a clean point. No nick. No flat. A cat with a sharper ear than our registry says it should have.

"Photograph," I said. Rafi did. Wide, mid, close, then a raked-light shot so the relief reads for people who need shadows to understand.

I set the registry card under the loupe and ran the lamp in a slow circle. Micro pitting sits like a constellation inside the cat and near the inner ring, tiny valleys where the die face carried grit the day it met paper. The photo in the archival sleeve from ten years ago maps those pits the way sailors map stars. Three near the cat's cheek. One cluster near the lower serif of the R in LIBRARY. A small string along the inner ring at five o'clock.

I brought the stamp head under the lamp and let the metal show me its own sky. Pits live in cast iron like freckles. You do not replicate a freckle map without cutting a new face. The head in my hand had pitting, yes, but the cheek cluster did not repeat as three. It read as two and a ghost. The lower serif cluster near the R was wider by a breath. The string at five o'clock broke after two and resumed a degree later, a skip that does not exist in the card photo. If the die wore down over a decade, the hills would soften and the valleys would shallow. They do not migrate. These had moved.

"Say it," Asa said, softer.

"Micro pitting on the face does not match the registry photo," I said. "We have two near the cheek where the card shows three. The cluster near the R has shifted. The string along the inner ring at five starts later. The outer ring bite is wider at eight and shy at two. The ear tip on this face is sharp. The registry ear shows a tiny flat from the restoration file."

Gran set a finger on the card where the tiny flat lives and nodded once.

I swung the lamp to low angle. The overlay helped, but the eye loves metal. I took the archive photo from the folder and put it side by side with the live face. Rafi set his phone on a little tripod and shot both for the record. The archive photo includes a ruler and a date. The date tells a story no mouth can spin away. I held the iron so the pitting lived where the photo's pitting lives. It did not. If a person wants to argue wear or dirt, they have to explain how a valley walks to a new home. Valleys do not travel.

"Scoring at the rim," I said. "Light polish marks here and here." I pointed to two faint striations near twelve and three, lines a buffer can leave when a careless hand tries to make a face look new. Those marks do not live on the registry card. They live on this metal under my lamp.

Asa let the lamp speak for a count of ten, then looked at Gran. "Tell me about the restoration," he said.

She kept her eyes on the card as she answered, not for effect, for respect.

"Ten years ago," she said, "the stamp left town for cleaning and stabilization. The die face had a burr at the ear and a nick at the ring near ten that kept snagging paper during the last run before the library moved. We sent it to Harper and Knoll in the city. They cleaned the face, corrected the burr, and set a micro nick at the ear when they dressed the edge. We photographed the face when it came home and pressed this card under controlled weight. That ear nick is the fingerprint. It is not here."

She tapped the task lamp base with one spare nail, the sound a little metronome for the room.

"Say the year," Asa said.

"Fifteen years into my retirement," she said. "Which makes it ten years back from today. We had the grant for encasement that winter. Harper and Knoll logged the work. They would still have the ticket."

Rafi had already opened a note for the call. He will track the conservator. He lives for phone trees.

I set the stamp head face up and brought the loupe nose-close again. If the ear carried no nick, then the ring near ten should also tell. The restoration sets can correct a burr but leave a diagnostic mark that lives in the registry photo like a tiny comet. I slid the loupe to ten and found no comet. The edge read smooth where the card shows a small bite.

"Registry shows a scar near ten," I said. "This face does not. The ear nick holds in the registry. This face shows a clean ear. The overlay and the micro pits disagree. That is three lanes of mismatch."

Rafi lifted the sponsor card sleeve from last night, the one with the pressure ghost circle and the small constellation inside. He held it next to the live bite on scrap. The ghost on the card showed a smooth ear. The pitting on that ghost, faint as it was, looked more like the face under my lamp than the card from ten years back. A lawyer will yell at me if I say the ghost proves the face, but we all saw the family resemblance.

Asa did not add poetry. He never does. He takes bad news like an accountant and sets it where it cannot slip.

"Chain," he said.

"Chain," I answered.

I wrote the test line in the binder in my square hand so a stranger who hates me can still read it. Ex-libris die pressed on scrap under lamp with foam support. Bite misaligns overlay by half a hair. Ear lacks restoration nick. Micro pitting differs from registry photo in three regions. Rim shows two light polish striations absent in archive image. I signed. Rafi signed as witness. Gran initialed the registry card sleeve. Asa dated the margin. Peppermint flicked his ear at my pen and sneezed once.

"Return the head," Asa said.

"Under the acrylic, same base," I said.

We did the march in reverse. I cradled the head on the towel. Rafi opened the office door. Gran wrote the carry time. We crossed the hall. Asa walked two steps behind me so the camera would read his shadow as responsibility. I set the head in its slot, centered, and closed the acrylic. I locked it. I held the key in view of the front camera, then dropped it in my pocket. The barium dust on the bow had shifted a touch. Enough to leave new proof on cloth if someone wants to get curious later and pretend the key lives in a bowl. It does not.

Back in the office, I let my hand rest flat on the desk. I do that when a fact lands so close to the line that people will try to kick it back. Give it a second to seat. Let your pulse fall. Then write the sentence that cleans up the room.

"The stamp under our vitrine does not match the town's restoration record," I said. "It presses without the ear nick. The pitting map disagrees. The ring's bite shifts half a hair from the standard. The face looks polished in two spots where the archive shows none. If this were a guitar, I would say it is the same shape and the same song in the wrong key."

Gran made a soft approving sound for the first time all morning. She keeps praise in a jar with a tight lid.

"Asa," I said, "you will call Harper and Knoll and ask for the ticket. You will ask for the photo they took when they shipped. We will give them our file number and this card. You will ask if any museum replicas left their shop with a face like this. They will say no, and then we will keep going anyway."

"I will ask for the shipping address on the return from ten years back," he said. "And for the courier who signed. We will follow that route and see if anyone swapped a head in a lobby for a head in a box."

"Celeste tried to stage access all day," I said. "Someone stamped a sponsor card by pressure, not ink, during that afternoon window. Your back door holds a press that swung at a head. Your router met a Chamber pool iPad at five fifty-eight and seven oh five. If the Chamber holds a replica, their inventory will look thinner when you ask."

"Who had Chamber tech after hours," he said, as if the router still sat in front of us.

"Same question sits on the stamp," I said. "Who had hands on this head after five."

We sat a long minute. The lamp hummed. The office clock clicked once when the minute turned. Peppermint found the little ray that sneaks under the blinds and warmed his spine. Texture only. He gives nothing to chain but time.

Gran set a finger on the registry card again and looked up at me with the face she uses when she knows I know the thing she is about to say.

"The original left town for restoration ten years ago," she said, calm as a ledger. "It returned with a nick at the ear you can see under any light. This one lacks it."

CHAPTER 8

Tote Fiber

The front room wore last night's order like armor. Brace strip on the bay. Cones two feet off the pane. Signs at eye level. The Founder's Table sat quiet, acrylic clean and locked. People still came to point and whisper because people will always choose a room with a story over a room without one.

I wanted the rug, the rack, and the track.

The coat rack stands to the right of the door, two steps from the guestbook stand, right where Celeste liked to plant herself and steer bodies. Yesterday she planted, argued, and made her case for optics while that red tote with its pins kept brushing our world. That corner collected lint like a magnet. Good. Lint remembers.

"Peppermint," I said, "hold the post."

He blinked on the register stool as if accepting a promotion to immovable object.

Rafi set the cart by the rack. He had the lint roller sleeves, tweezers, glassine, the small loupe, and our pocket microscope that turns a phone into a lab for people who accept limits. Gran opened the witness ledger on the counter and wrote the time. 9:18 a.m., coat rack and lobby rug collection.

I knelt at the rug edge where the rack's shadow lies by noon.

The pile there had a faint wave from foot traffic and bag drags. I rolled the lint lift slow along the border, one swipe per strip, no overlap. First pass caught sand, papery dust, one blue polyester hair, two cat hairs I refused to identify, and a short, glossy red filament that wanted to ride the static right back into the rug.

"Hello," I said. I lifted it with tweezers and set it onto glassine.

Rafi slid the strip into a sleeve and labeled it. Rug edge, rack corner, pass 1, 9:20. He put the red filament in a second sleeve. I wrote a small card for the binder. Short red filament recovered at rug edge near rack, consistent with nylon by sheen. I did not write match. Not yet.

I ran a second pass three inches farther into the room, same slow drag. Another red filament clung to the tape, longer, kinked at one end where it had snagged on something sharper than wool. Into a sleeve it went. Rug edge, rack corner, pass 2, 9:22.

Third pass, nothing red, all dust and a foil confetti star I did not need. Rafi logged it anyway because he hates gaps.

"Rack," I said.

Rafi held the base steady while I swabbed the lower hook bracket with a clean cotton tip, not to lift DNA, to catch any loose threads where bags swing. The swab came up with three pale fuzzes and one red feather-sliver that broke when I teased it. Nylon will do that when it is cheap and tired. Back into the glassine. Labeled. Logged.

"Lanyards," I said.

The Chamber had left a small spare bundle in their tote yesterday. We still had it in a bag they forgot to ask for because forgetting to ask for things is a Chamber skill. I pulled one red strap free and held it under the lamp. Woven nylon, medium denier, rectangular clasp with a spring gate and a little cat-shaped charm they hand out like candy. The clasp edge showed a bright bite where plating had rubbed to base. A lanyard lives rough. It tells you nothing unless it goes where it should not and leaves a mark. Yesterday it did.

"Front track," I said.

The bay's interior track at the bottom keeps the pane from rattling and lets us seat the frame for winter. Yesterday I stared at the crack origin and forgot to lean into the track where metal thieves love to leave first. Today I bent with the loupe and raked the task lamp along the inner. The paint showed normal scuffs and one fresh crescent at knee height that did not live there last week when I cleaned the track with a cloth and language Gran does not like in front of kids. The crescent had the right width for a spring gate. The bright underbite told fresh removal of finish. Two shallow parallel ticks trailed it like claws. I did not need poetry. I needed a photo.

"Scale," I said.

Rafi set the scale card against the inner track. I braced the lamp so the crescent threw a shadow. He took three frames, then one macro with the clip-on lens. He exhaled once and nodded. The camera had it.

I lined the spare lanyard's clasp up to the crescent. The curve matched. The width matched. The angle of the spring gate matched the ticks. I did not touch the track with the clasp. I held the match in air.

"Say it," Gran said from the counter.

"Interior track shows a fresh scrape consistent with a spring clasp like the Chamber volunteer lanyard," I said. "Crescent width lines. Parallel ticks line. Height lines with bag swing. That sits right where the crack bloomed after the stand bumped."

"Inside out," she said. "Like yesterday."

"Inside out," I said.

I set the lanyard on the mat and took two photos of its gate, one closed, one open. Plating flaked at the edge. The flake bright matched the bright at the track. That is not proof. It is a relationship. People are the ones who insist on marriage. I settle for family resemblance until lab says vows.

I pulled the two red filaments from the rug and the two we took from the sill yesterday, lined them on white under the phone microscope, and brought their skin into the frame. Round cross-section, not flattened. Dye even, no heather. Fray pattern at the broken end showed hot-cut signs on two and a true break on one. The sheen under the lamp sat the same. The color read the same across four, a clean red that falls between cherry and school strap, the color marketing teams call simple.

"Vendor does nylon straps by contract," Rafi said. "Chamber buys in bulk from a printer on the highway. People throw them away after three events. Some keep them like trophies."

"Some toss fibers like confetti," I said.

I wrote three labels for the sleeves. Rug-1, Rug-2, Sill-1, Sill-2. I kept them separate because blending helps no one. I slid the four into a flat in the binder and set a big dot next to the entry for the lanyard scrape with a note to ask the glazier if the track finish we lost measures clean under his light. He will give us the millage. He loves that.

Rafi brought me the elbow-height measure where a bag corner swings if a person thinks they are narrower than they are. I measured from the floor to the crescent scrape. Thirty-two inches. I measured from the floor to the center of the rack's lower hook, the one Celeste banged into with her tote twice while she was trying to charm a donor. Thirty-three. You will never get a line as straight as your heart wants. You settle for numbers that live because the room makes them live.

I wrote: Track scrape height 32 inches. Rack lower hook 33 inches. Scrape arc shows match to spring clasp profile from Chamber lanyard. Red nylon filament at rug edge and sill share sheen and dye under phone scope. Not a lab match. A clerk's link.

Asa stepped in from the hall and saw the lined sleeves and the bright crescent on the track. He had not slept much. He had the calm face he wears when he is about to ask me to say my sentence again into a recorder so he can save me from a courtroom later.

"Give it to me," he said.

"Celeste argued by the rack," I said. "Her volunteer's lanyard and tote brushed the area. The rug says so. The rack says so. The bay took a hit from inside. A spring clasp scraped the interior track. The red nylon on the sill and the red nylon here behave the same. Yesterday that room carried this fiber."

"Clasp scrape explains the ping before the crack," he said.

"Yes," I said. "That little metallic kiss Darren heard could be a clasp flicking the track before the stand hit. It is a sound people mistake for a soft chime."

Asa lifted his pen. "He said chime," he said.

"He did," I said. "We had the back door chime at 6:19 too. He works a lane with wheels. He may hear both and choose a word that feels right. This scrape says one thing cut paint here while we watched donors act careful. The bump after made the pane speak. Order matters."

Gran wrote that slowly as if carving.

Rafi fished a lint filament from the back of the volunteer lanyard bundle and put it under the phone scope next to Rug-2. Same dye. Same sheen. The microscope is not a lab but it is a fair mirror. I let the image live on the screen and took a shot for the folder.

We did not need more from the rug. I ran one last lint lift along the guestbook stand leg where Celeste moved the book at six. One tiny red hair flared and stuck to the tape near a faint line of chalk dust I had left when I traced shoes last night. I cut the tape square and slid it onto a small slide. People think tapeslift belong in crime shows. They belong in binders that do not lie.

"Who is on the Chamber's volunteer list for yesterday," Asa said.

"Two names," I said. "Marsi Jenk at ten to four, then Gavin Voss at four to five forty. Toby dropped pins at five forty-five and left at six oh two. Celeste had her hands on everything all day."

"Get me those lanyards," he said.

"They are here," I said. "They left the bundle."

"Who signed for them," he said.

"Chamber pool," I said. "No personal tags."

He set his jaw at that and looked at the scrape again. He smiled with only one corner of his mouth. It does not mean joy. It means his book will have a page titled People Who Pretend Tools Do Not Have Owners.

Peppermint stepped off the stool and walked to the bay. He sat and stared at the crescent scrape with a level of attention he usually gives moths. He blinked twice at the bright and then turned to the rack and blinked once. I did not clap for him. He does not work for me.

Martin Keene walked in at ten twenty with a face that wanted to sound helpful and a blazer that wanted people to trust it. He is on the Chamber board, a man who writes quotes for the paper and calls them statements. He had been in and out yesterday, hovering, adjusting, approving his own presence. Today he came to tidy a narrative.

"Terrible," he said, soft enough to be heard, loud enough to be recorded by whoever wanted it. "We are all shocked."

"Keep your tote away from the track," I said, and pointed at the crescent without smiling.

He stopped. He laughed in a way that expected a smile. He did not get one.

"I am here to help," he said. "I spoke with Celeste at six oh five last night on my way out. She said she was leaving and would meet us at the hall. I can confirm she left then. You will want that on the record."

"You spoke with her at six oh five," I said.

"Yes," he said. "She was at the front. She turned toward Oak. She told me to lock the Chamber case. I did. I left."

He said it like a man who likes a clean sentence more than a true one.

I looked at the front camera monitor in the office doorway where the screen still slept. I did not wake it yet. I looked at Gran. She did not blink.

"At six oh five," I said, "Celeste wrote her name twice in my guestbook. Then she moved it with her palm, signed again, and patted it. At six twelve someone reprinted a donation slip she had already taken. At six nineteen the back chime sounded. At six twenty-one I called time at the door."

"I can only speak to my memory," he said, and switched to the tone people use when they intend to be condescending and miscalculate their audience. "It was around six. I am sure of it. She left."

"We have cameras," I said.

He lifted his hands, palms out, generous. "By all means," he said. "Check them."

He smiled again in a way he uses at podiums. Rafi woke the monitor and called up the front bay angle with the time bar from five fifty to seven. He scrubbed to six forty and froze the frame where the brace strip catches light and the cones throw their shadows. A silhouette stood in the street-side glow, right at the pane, the same slim height, the same cut of blazer, the same tote strap thrown long across a shoulder. You could not see the face. You could see the shape through braced glass.

"Six forty," I said.

Martin looked at the screen and did not move his mouth. His eyes did a small calculus and then landed on indignation the way a toddler lands on a couch. He chose it because it was soft.

"That could be anyone," he said. "Many women in this town own that blazer, I am sure."

"Many women in this town do not carry a Chamber tote with pins arranged that way," I said. "But I am not asking you to identify her. I am telling you your statement lands wrong. If you saw Celeste leave at six oh five, then at six forty someone stood at my glass with her silhouette. Which means your memory belongs in quotes, not in ink."

"I am only trying to help," he said again. The words always sound worse the second time.

"Help by giving me a list of who had keys to the Chamber hall," I said. "Help by giving me the sign-out for pool devices. Help by giving me the inventory number for the lanyards you handed out yesterday." I tapped the bundle. "Help by telling me why a pool iPad named CR-iPad joined our Guest at five fifty-eight and seven oh five."

He did not like that I knew names. He smoothed his tie and looked at Asa. Asa did not smile at him. He has a gift for not smiling for long stretches.

"Officer," Martin said, with polite gravity, "I will have our administrator email your office with any documentation you require."

"You will bring it on paper," Asa said. "Before lunch."

Martin remembered his calendar and nodded. He still wanted to own a sentence.

"I maintain," he said, "that I saw Celeste leave at six oh five."

"Then your day and the camera disagree," I said. "One of them will win."

He looked at the crescent scrape again, at the cones, at the brace, at the cat who blinked at him like a metronome. He opened his mouth, closed it, and chose to go.

After he left, the room held the kind of quiet that feels like someone let more air into the ductwork. Rafi turned the monitor back to the associations log he likes to keep up like a fish tank. No new blips. The three lines on the printout above the printer stayed in their little row like a family that refuses to sit apart.

I went back to the rug and rolled one more lift along the baseboard. Nothing red. Good. I would have worried about finding a ribbon's worth. The point is not volume. The point is placement. A filament here, a filament there, the scrape in the track, the scrape on the sill, the two six oh fives, the reprint, the pool iPad, the press with a foot that wore the front lane. None of these alone is more than a nudge. Together they start to stand.

Peppermint chose the sun strip beside the cones and lay with his spine along the line like a ruler. He watched the door. He did not look at the monitor. He does not need screens. He has a sense of traffic.

Gran shut the witness ledger and tapped it twice with the back of her nails. Tap, tap. It is how she tells me to breathe. I did.

"Next," she said.

"Next we call the printer on the highway and ask about the Chamber lanyard order," I said. "We ask if they changed vendors this quarter. We ask if they had a batch with weak weave that sheds at the edges. We ask if any new lots went out yesterday."

"Then you bring me a coffee," she said.

"Then I bring you a coffee," I said.

Rafi printed the still of the six forty silhouette and slid it into a sleeve with the time stamp burned in the lower corner. He drew a thin pencil line along the tote strap and the pins. He did not add labels. He knows I will. He wrote the caption on a blank strip for me. Front bay, 6:40 p.m., silhouette with tote.

Asa read the line on the witness ledger and then looked at me.

"Martin can be wrong without being a liar," he said.

"Yes," I said. "And he can be a liar without knowing it. Today I do not need to add him to any list except the one that says he wants the day to look tidy."

He put the printout of the three lines into his notebook and clipped the silhouette still behind it. He likes to nest paper so that when he opens it later, the room steps back into his hands. He left us the lanyard scrape and the rug sleeves and a day with plenty left to say.

I took the spare lanyard clasp and held it near the track, not touching, another air match to the crescent. When you see an object line up with a mark in the world, your brain wants to declare victory. I do not grant it. I grant enough to keep going.

"Red nylon," I said, writing it on a card. "Track scrape. Silhouette at 6:40."

"End your note with a period," Gran said.

I did. And then I wrote the question that would carry the next chapter into shape.

If Celeste left at 6:05, whose silhouette did my camera catch at 6:40.

CHAPTER 9

Key Custody

Counters talk if you let them. Ours had three things that mattered this morning. A key cup with one brass barrel and a bowed head dusted last week with a whisper of barium from my kit. The guestbook box we put back on the counter to work under camera. The lock log clipboard I keep next to the till like a bad habit.

Gran opened the witness ledger and wrote the time. 10:06 a.m., counter audit, stamp case key, guestbook, lock log. She underlined counter. She knows where fights start.

Rafi brought the tray with gloves, a low-angle lamp, lint cloth, the small UV, and tape lifts. Peppermint settled on the register stool, tail wrapped like a seal, eyes on the key cup. He likes small metal things and the attention people give them. Texture, not help.

"We start with the log," I said. "Then the metal."

The lock log is a simple clipboard with a simple rule. If a key leaves the cup, a hand writes a line. If a lock opens, a hand writes a line. Yesterday shows four lines. 8:42 a.m., vitrine opened under witness for bite test, key to office by LW, witnessed by GW, AQ. 8:56 a.m., vitrine closed and locked, key returned. 6:00 p.m., closing prep, vitrine checked, no access. 6:50 p.m., post-incident check, seal intact.

No entry after six. No one wrote their name in the log to take the key. That matters. It will matter more when a lawyer tries to say the room was chaos. The room keeps receipts.

"Key next," Asa said from the hall. He stood where the camera caught his face without catching his hands. He trusts my counter more than his.

I pulled on nitriles and lifted the key by the ring with tweezers, not because it is fragile, because I like cutting down noise. The head wore the same faint chalk I put on it last week. Barium in a carrier that barely clings. It transfers like a thin pastry dust if a thumb hunts it. The trick is to tag the thing you do not want walked. If someone walks it anyway, their ridges become generous.

I set the key on a clean glass tile under the lamp and tilted the cone. The head lit with that matte kiss I know. I rotated until the carrier filed out every shallow ridge it met. Two clean ridge sets rode the bow in miniature. Mine. And one other. No crowd of party prints. No smeared chorus. Two. The second set ran narrower, a bit tighter at the delta, the center of the print. The bow showed two lift-and-place arcs, not a long sweat press. Someone pinched, maybe turned the key a hair, then set it down.

"Photograph," I said.

Rafi took a run of shots. Full key, head close, raked light to catch ridge relief, then a scale with the center of the pattern. He did not talk. I like him most when he does not talk.

I touched the tiniest breath of magnetic powder to the bow, just enough to make the ridges pick up a little shadow. The second print bloomed. A right thumb. Shallow ridge height, narrow flow. Not proof of a person. Proof of not me.

"Say it," Asa said.

"Barium dust I placed last week sits on the head," I said. "Two ridge sets on the bow. Mine, from this morning when I carried it to the office. One other, consistent with a right thumb pinch placed after my barium dust went on, which was last week. No other full prints on the head."

"Lift it," he said.

I did two tape lifts, one over my ridge set where it crossed the top arc, one over the narrow set at the side. I slid each to a clear film card and wrote Key head, ridge set A, LW, and Key head, ridge set B, unknown. I signed and Gran initialed. Rafi logged the photo numbers.

Peppermint flicked his ear and looked pointedly at the guestbook box. I obliged him with a look of my own.

We took the guestbook out of the box and set it on the counter where it lives. The small strip marker Gran tucked at Chapter 4 still sat at the two 6:05 entries. I did not open there. I opened two pages later and set the lamp to a shallow rake. The spine shows everything you drag over it. The varnish takes a mark and keeps it if the world is kind.

At about mid-spine, a faint diagonal ran from the lower left toward the upper right. Barely there. A chalky film no one would notice unless they loved dull things. I tilted the lamp and the line bloomed for a breath, then went quiet again. Right where a key bow would ride if someone had swept it across while shifting the book out of her way.

"Scale," I said.

Rafi placed the millimeter strip and shot the diagonal with the same patience he gives bookplates. He took one more with the UV. It did not glow like the citrus. It dulled under that light, as barium carrier will sometimes do. The important part lived in my head and the witness ledger. I wrote: Faint matte transfer across guestbook spine, consistent with barium carrier from key head.

"Check the time," Asa said.

We pulled the front camera clip to the counter tablet and scrubbed to 6:10. The angle shows the counter from the door. Celeste by the rack at 6:02. Celeste writing at 6:05, then closing the guestbook with the palm of her left hand. At 6:14 she returns to the counter, pivots the book, slides it three inches for a "flow" line she makes with her body. Her right hand dips toward the key cup, not a grab, a graze. She talks with her face toward the door and her hand rests on the counter. The key in the cup rocks. You can see the ring spin a quarter. Then her hand lifts. She drags the book a last inch. The spine crosses a chalk dust frame you do not see on camera, the one I now read under the lamp. She pats the cover, turns, and watches the room like a person who has done a small thing she thinks is smart.

"Time," I said. "6:15."

Gran wrote exactly that on the witness line. Guestbook spine shows faint transfer line, 6:15, camera places Celeste moving book at that moment, hand grazes key cup.

"Asa," I said, "you will ask for a fingerprint tech to lift the ridge from the guestbook spine if you want it. The carrier is weak. We might get nothing. The photograph lands enough for me."

"For me too," he said. "For a judge, we bring both."

I went back to the key. The head still wore the two ridge sets. I put the lifts side by side under the phone scope so I could hold them in my eye while I watched the camera frame of her hand on the cup. I matched nothing to Celeste without a proper comparator. I matched the behavior. Pinch and replace. Small graze of a bow across a book spine, chalk kiss left behind, barium from my kit.

We checked the smart lock log on the back door while the counter was open, because logs love company. Asa's warrant had landed overnight. He had the file. 18:01 unlock by code 04. Conrad's code. Lock again at 18:03. No events on the stamp case. That lock is dumb and lives by key only. Which brings us back to the cup.

"Who had the key last," Asa said.

"Me," I said. "Eight fifty-six. I locked the vitrine and put the key in the cup. Gran watched. Rafi filmed my hands without needing to be told. No one signed it out after. The camera shows Celeste brush the cup at 6:15. The bow rides the book. The spine carries the line."

"Who handles the guestbook most," he said.

"Gran," I said. "Me. Paula, our regular who likes to fuss about flow when the room gets tight. She lifts the book by the spine and tucks it under the stand when she thinks people will knock it."

"Bring her," he said.

Paula is always here by morning coffee. She writes the blocks on the community board with her neat teacher script. She came to the counter with a paper cup and a face I trust to remember where people stood.

"You moved the guestbook last night," I said.

"I did," she said. "At six fifteen, maybe, I pulled it an inch so people would stop crowding the map stand."

"Why," I said.

"Celeste asked," she said. "She said it would improve flow. She had that lanyard swinging and her tote bumping every elbow in town, so I humored her. I slid the book across the mat. I did not touch your key."

"Did she," I said.

"She put her hand on the cup and then on the book," Paula said. "Like this." Paula set her hand near the cup and slid her palm across the spine. She did not touch the key. Her hand would have brushed the head if the cup had been half an inch closer. In the camera still, it was.

I pointed to the faint line. Paula leaned and squinted.

"I did not make that," she said. "She did."

Gran wrote her sentence in the witness ledger. Paula says Celeste moved guestbook "to improve flow" at that time, hand near key cup.

Paula looked at Asa because she likes her sentences to reach the right ears. "She wanted your stamp," Paula said. "She had a look like a crow at a shiny thing."

"Noted," he said.

Rafi pulled the older clip from 5:59 when Celeste did a similar maneuver. At that time the book sits closer to the edge. Her hand sweeps, the key in the cup stays still. No line on the spine at that moment. I froze 5:59, then 6:15, and put both frames side by side on the tablet. In the second, the key ring turns a quarter when her hand touches the cup. A tiny movement the naked eye would miss in a crowd. The camera is cruel. It forgets grace.

"Lock log supports you," Asa said. "Key not signed out. Key moved just enough to kiss the book. Two prints on the head. We will see if the lab can read the second ridge."

Rafi put the ridge lift B into a rigid sleeve for the tech. He writes the time. He writes the place. He writes his initials like a person who learned from watching me get scolded one winter when I forgot to initial a slide and paid for it in an affidavit. Small scars teach.

I checked the key slot in the acrylic base under the vitrine again while the room breathed. The brass barrel showed a faint fresher arc at the entry where the bow had scraped the inner edge during yesterday's sanctioned test. No new scars after that. The seal on the acrylic sat intact. The face under the acrylic had not grown a nick overnight. My body let some breath go.

Back at the counter I ran a clean tape lift along the spine where the line showed, not to get prints, to lift whatever carrier sat on the varnish. The adhesive took a tiny veil of chalk. Under the scope, the lift showed a diffuse dust with a brightness like river silt. I took a control lift from a clean patch and saw nothing. That is all I needed for my day. The lab can say barium if they want later. I wrote chalk veil consistent with prior tag.

"Who else touched the cup," Asa said.

"Gavin at five ten," Rafi said. "He dumped coins in it by mistake and I told him to stop being unhelpful. He laughed and moved on. His hand did not touch the head. He hates touching anything with purpose."

That is Gavin.

"Print the frame sequence from 6:14 to 6:16," Asa said.

Rafi did. He set four stills in a sleeve, time burned in the corner. Celeste hand near cup. Ring pivots. Palm slides book. Palm lifts. Celeste turns. I wrote the times underneath so my future self will thank me.

Peppermint hopped down, took two steps, and put a paw on the guestbook corner like a notary, then turned and flicked his tail at the key cup. He watched it look back.

"Who else knew you dusted the key," Asa said.

"Gran and Rafi," I said. "I do that sort of thing in the open. It keeps honest people honest and someone else clumsy."

"Barium on a key is not a secret," Gran said. "We used to do it on the archive cabinet when the high school docents came to help. They learned not to fidget quick."

Asa nodded. He does not enjoy tricks. He approves of markers that make the world leave footprints.

I set the lock log on the mat and wrote Key custody challenged at counter. Then I read the last of the lines out loud for the camera that watches my hands so my voice will live next to my pen. Two entries at 6:05 by Celeste, reprint at 6:12, guestbook moved at 6:15 with hand at key cup, back chime at 6:19, body at 6:21. Short chain. Clean stairs.

"Ask Paula again," Asa said, "what words Celeste used."

Paula thought for half a breath. "Improve flow," she said. "She said it twice. First at five fifty-nine. Then again just after six. She was pointing with her hand in a way that told me she had no idea how rooms work."

"She knows optics," I said.

"She chases them," Paula said.

"Thank you," Asa said to her, and meant it.

Paula went back to her bulletin board with her cup and her pen and a look on her face that told me she was filing woe under a quiet anger that fits a teacher better than a politician. I like her better every year.

Rafi printed the one-page summary and pinned it above the printer next to the three lines from the router page. It looks orderly. Lines make sense to him. It helps me breathe.

Asa closed his notebook and tapped it with his finger. "Two prints on the key," he said. "Your dust line on the book at 6:15. Paula puts Celeste's hand there at that time. Lock log says no access. Case stays locked until your test this morning. That ends this question for me."

"Good," I said.

He gave me the only hook I wanted. "Now I go ask the Chamber who else puts their hands in other people's cups," he said, and walked toward the door.

Gran shut the witness ledger and placed her palm on the cover for a second. It is her way of blessing a page. Peppermint blinked once, then turned his head to the bay. The brace glowed. The crescent scrape on the track stayed bright under the morning. Everything said the same thing if you stood in the right place and listened.

Key. Book. Line. Time.

And when Paula looked back at me from the board, she added one more sentence, simple as sugar.

"She moved the guestbook," Paula said, "to improve flow."

CHAPTER 10

Till and Time

Machines don't care about stories. They write numbers and stop. That is why I like them.

We started at the espresso till because it prints truth even when no one wants a latte. Gran opened the witness ledger and wrote the time. 10:42 a.m., till audit, receipt roll, camera sync. Rafi brought the toolkit and the small pry bar we use to pop a stubborn printer door. Peppermint curled on the stool and set his chin on the register rail like a foreman.

The till lives in its own island, a step from the donation printer and two from the guestbook stand. I turned the key to report mode and ran the audit list for yesterday from 5:30 to 6:30. The thermal chittered and pushed out a curl of paper with the line codes that make most people glaze over. I read them like a road map.

"Mark the window," I said.

Rafi laid a clear ruler across the strip and drew two light pencil ticks at 18:11 and 18:12 so my eye wouldn't wander. The tape carried three entries that mattered and a lot that did not. I read the three aloud.

"18:11:36 RBK LAST," I said. "18:12:02 VOID SLIP 0174," I said. "18:12:05 PRINT SLIP 0174 COP."

RBK means rollback. The till printed the last slip again without opening a sale. VOID means someone voided a slip entry on the donation stream. The COP flag belongs to our donation printer when it spits a top copy with no tender. All three lined up. A person touched the system at 6:11 and 6:12 to replay and then void. Then the donation printer reprinted 174 without money. The printer log in the router file told the same story in a different accent.

"Read the donation log slice," I said.

Rafi pulled up the print service export he saved. 18:12:04 Donation_Slip_174 Reprint True. Time stamp married the till's 18:12:05 COP. Two clocks, one minute, one action.

Gran wrote the three codes in the ledger, then drew a small bracket and wrote Reprint window between them. She underlined the word window once. It helps later.

"Camera," I said.

The front overhead gives us a clean angle on the island. We scrubbed to 6:10 and let it play. At 6:10:58 I was across the room with a donor. Gran stood by the bay cones. Rafi was in the back hall with Asa. No clerk hands anywhere near the island. At 6:11:36 the espresso till woke and printed an RBK. No body in frame. The donation printer stayed quiet. At 6:12:02 the till spit a VOID on the audit strip. Three seconds later the donation printer fed a single sheet. No hand on either machine. On the corner of the wide frame a shoulder crossed and vanished. Sleeve, dark, smooth. Not ours.

"Angle two," I said.

Rafi flipped to the side camera that watches the island from the office doorway. The shoulder lived there for a breath. A person stood just outside the boundary of the island, reached in, tapped the RBK key with two fingers, tapped VOID, then stepped back toward the guest chair as if waiting for a friend. The body never faced the lens. The hand wore no rings. A watch flashed once. The band looked like a leather strap with a narrow keeper. My staff do not wear that watch. Celeste did. The angle caught the strap for half a blink.

"Print that still," I said.

Rafi froze at 6:11:36 and printed the frame that held the hand over the RBK key. He printed 6:12:02 for the VOID tap. He printed 6:12:05 when the donation printer fed. He wrote each time under each still and slid them in a sleeve. His pencil line connected them without arrows.

"The till wrote it," I said. "Rollback of last. Void. Donation copy."

"Last was 174," Gran said. "At 5:48."

"Correct," I said. "She took the top. At 6:12 she wanted another top without money on our books. The RBK and VOID kept our drawer clean while she fed her pocket."

"Who is she," Asa said from the hall.

"The person who stood half a step out of frame and reached in," I said. "The strap is a tell. I won't hang a name on a wrist. I'll hang a name on a pattern when your phone pulls it from hers."

Asa nodded. He does not fight with clocks. He writes them.

I tore the audit strip clean and taped it above the island for the day. People ask fewer questions when paper answers first.

"Now the ring," I said.

We keep a tempered glass sheet on the counter where we fill sponsor cards. It wipes clean if you keep an eye on it. Yesterday turned the eye to other things. Today the eye went back to the surface.

I wiped the glass with a dry cloth and then held the task lamp at a low angle. A faint circle lived in the lower right quadrant where a thoughtless cup once sat. Not wet. Not sticky. A ghost. The ring carried a nick at the edge like a cup with a chip. I measured the diameter. Eight centimeters, a hair under. The nick sat at about twenty degrees off the top.

"Photograph," I said.

Rafi shot it with the scale in frame and kept the rake shallow.

He tilted and shot again so the notch showed. I took three blank sponsor cards from the stack and held them under the lamp. On card seven from the top, a faint ring lived at the same size and nick position. Card eleven carried it too. Card thirteen, again. All three too faint for ink. All three born from pressure, not spill. If you lay a card on a copier glass with a ring shadow sealed to it, your copy will carry that ghost. If you stamp that copy with a die, the pressure can grab the ghost and make it yours. We had one card in a sleeve with a pressure circle and a notch from last night. Now we had three with a coffee ring ghost near the corner where the Chamber likes to print sponsor name plates for events.

"Not our glass," I said.

Rafi lifted our copier cover and cleaned the glass with a cloth. We keep it clean like a cutting board. No rings. No nick. No old coffee. The habit makes today simple. The ghost on our cards did not come from our machine.

"Pull the Chamber copier image," I said.

He already had the thought. He opened his photo roll and scrolled to last month when the Chamber asked for extra flyers and he walked across with a flash drive because their email chokes. He had shot a quick frame of their copier to send a note about the cover being loose. The photo showed the glass, the white lid open, and a wide ring with a nick in the upper right where someone parked a cup last winter and never cleaned the shadow. He put that old photo under our phone scope next to a new shot he requested from Asa's patrol, who walked over ten minutes ago to take a fresh one. The new image showed the same ring, same nick, same position on the glass. The old coffee had never been removed. The copier wears other people's laziness like jewelry.

"Overlay," I said.

Rafi printed the Chamber glass photo to scale and the faint ring from our sponsor card from last night. He cut a transparent circle overlay to match our card ring. He laid it over the Chamber glass photo and rotated until the nick fell on the nick. It lined. He set the same overlay on the ring photo from our counter glass. The nick did not line. Our counter nick sits at twenty degrees and small. The Chamber glass ring sits at thirty-five degrees and thicker. The sponsor cards carry the thicker ring.

"Say it clean," Gran said.

"Three sponsor cards carry a coffee ring ghost at a diameter and notch angle that match the Chamber copier glass, not our counter," I said. "Our counter ring is smaller and oriented different. The ghost traveled from their machine to our cards."

Asa nodded again. He does not waste approval. He wrote Chamber glass ring in his book and marked it with a dot the way Gran does.

I went back to the island and looked at the audit strip again because I like to let numbers settle twice. 18:11:36 RBK LAST. 18:12:02 VOID SLIP 0174. 18:12:05 PRINT SLIP 0174 COP. The times sit right between Celeste's second six oh five signature and Darren's chime at 6:19. A person stepped in, hit the keys, printed her copy, and then went to the hall door for the last minutes of her day.

"Who else knows the RBK shortcut," Rafi said.

"Me," I said. "Gran. Paula. Staff. We teach no volunteers. We post no cheat sheet. If a Chamber hand reached over and hit RBK and VOID, she learned it here before this week or carries muscle memory from running donation stations. Celeste liked showing she knew our toys."

Gran brought the sponsor stack and set the three ghosted cards in a row. She tilted her head like a bird and tapped each with a nail. The tiny nick showed in the same place on each. Not exact. Enough.

"They ran a batch at the Chamber office," she said. "They brought blanks here. They meant to swap when the show began."

"Then doubled down at 6:12," I said.

We pulled the camera clip from the Chamber's foyer off the city link, because Asa has that power. At 5:22 Celeste stood at their copier with the lid open, cup on the edge, one hand on a stack of cream cards. Toby handed her a sleeve. The photo shows the ring on the glass and the nick near the edge. They ran cards. They never wiped the ring. Later, under our light, the ring told on them.

Rafi printed the frame. Not a perfect face shot. Enough of a shoulder. Enough of a sleeve. Enough of that leather watch strap. He slid it behind the still of the hand over RBK.

"Keep yourself honest," I said.

"I am," he said. "The strap is in two places."

We took one last look at the donation printer queue. It showed the same reprint flag at 6:12 we had already printed. We added a note to the file to grab the spool file from the machine for the chain. We know what the pages will say. We print them because a court likes the complete folder.

"Count the sponsor stack," Gran said.

I counted. Fifteen blanks. Three with the ring ghost. One in the sleeve with the pressure circle from the stamp test. That makes nineteen cards in play. Our Chamber file says they promised twenty donors a card on the table last night. Someone took one with a ring. It will surface in a tote or a blazer pocket. I wrote a line to remind myself to ask Asa to watch for it when he opens boxes at their office.

Peppermint stood and stretched and put a paw on the audit strip like he wanted to bless it. He pulled back and looked impressed with himself. Texture, not help.

I logged the whole sequence in the binder with one of those long sentences that make jurors drowsy and save you later. At 18:11 the till printed RBK LAST without a sale. At 18:12 it printed VOID SLIP 0174 without tender. At 18:12 the donation printer reprinted 174 as a top copy. Camera shows a hand reach from the aisle to the RBK and VOID keys. Strap watch flash consistent with Celeste. No clerk present at island. Sponsor cards show coffee ring ghost that matches Chamber copier glass ring in diameter and nick orientation. Our counter ring does not match that ghost.

Asa took the page and read it. He did not change a word. He slid it back into the binder and set his finger on the line about the ring.

"Proof that the cards came from their shop," he said.

"Proof that at least three did," I said. "Enough for intent if you want it."

"I want it," he said.

He stepped into the hall and made the call to his patrol. His voice stayed low and precise. Ask Chamber staff to stand by their copier. Photograph the glass. Bag any sponsor stock with ring ghosts in the top twenty. Print the log from their donation iPad cart. The word iPad sat like a nail in a board.

I watched the island and thought about how often that corner has hosted hands that think machines are LOUD, so they won't get caught. Machines are not loud. They are patient.

Gran set a cup on a coaster on the service shelf and smirked at me when I looked at the ring. Her coffee never leaves a mark. I love that about her.

"Put it in one line," she said.

"At 6:11 and 6:12, the till and the donation printer locked the micro-timeline to a reprint of slip 174," I said. "Three sponsor cards carry a coffee ring ghost that matches the Chamber copier, not our counter. The hand that hit RBK and VOID did so without standing behind the island."

She wrote it in the ledger with her square hand so it would outlive us both.

Rafi taped the three stills for RBK, VOID, COP under the audit strip. He taped the Chamber glass ring photo next to the card ghost overlay. The board looked like a school lesson, which is

STACKS, STAMPS, AND SMOKE

how I like it. People came to the counter to ask what had happened. We pointed at the board and watched them nod. Numbers soothe the part of the brain that hates rumors.

Peppermint hopped down, walked to the bay, and sat facing the glass with the brace strip. He looked at the faint crescent scrape we saved from Chapter 8 and blinked twice. He approved of that ring too. He is honest. He likes shapes.

Asa came back from the call and asked one question without dressing it.

"You can swear that ring ghost is not from here," he said.

"Yes," I said. "Our copier glass is clean. The ghost on our counter glass is smaller with a different nick. The sponsor card ghost matches the Chamber glass. We have scale. We have a photo from last month. We have a fresh photo from five minutes ago. You can lay the three on the light box and see the notches land."

He nodded, let out a breath he holds for details, and looked at the hand over the RBK still.

"The strap," he said.

"The strap," I said.

He left to meet the Chamber administrator with the photo in his pocket and his voice already even. I watched him go and felt the shop settle another notch. We had the minute. We had the slip. We had the ring.

Machines tell the time. People try to bend it. The till laughed and printed its line. The copier laughed and left its ring where Celeste put her cup. Numbers stacked until they started to feel like a ladder.

I pressed the tape down flat on the wall. I like order. I like how it looks when a story tries to wriggle and the strip says no.

Then Rafi's phone buzzed. He glanced at the screen and held it up. A photo from Asa. Chamber copier glass, fresh, nick and all. He sent a second frame. A sponsor card on their counter with the same ghost circle in the same corner. He sent a third. A box of blank cards with a sticky that read, in Celeste's quick hand, "For tonight."

"Match," Rafi said.

"Match," I said.

The room felt cleaner. The day got shorter. The work got simple. The ghost ring on our cards came from their machine, not here.

CHAPTER 11

Alley Cam

Across the alley, the title office keeps hours, files, and a camera pointed at our back door. Practical people do practical things. Today that helps.

Rafi and I crossed with a clean drive and two sleeves. The clerk at the title office, Annie, knows us, knows Asa, and knows why chain matters. She walked us to the monitor, checked her wall clock, and set her system time next to ours. Their overlay runs one minute fast. We logged the offset, wrote it in the witness ledger, and did not touch the mouse until she said go.

"Pull six forty-five to seven fifteen," I said.

She scrubbed and set the loop. The angle takes in the mouth of the alley, our door, the stretch under the gutter, and the base of our back rack through the glass if the light catches it. The view sees shape, not faces. Good enough.

At 6:56 p.m., two delivery bikes slip past, no stop. At 6:57:48, a shadow crosses the distant light and becomes a person at the near edge, a clean figure in profile against the silver siding of the title office. Shoulder tote. We all lean in. The overlay reads 6:58:10, which puts it at 6:57:10 on our clock. The figure pauses at the line where the gutter drips, shifts the strap, and waits for breath. No face. The tote shows in a shallow angle, canvas with enamel pins clustered near the top seam. Two charms catch light. A gap shows where a small star would live if it were still attached. The gap is not a hole. You can read a ghost ring where pins rub fabric and leave a halo. The halo carries a tiny spike at one point, the point a star would make.

"Freeze and magnify," I said.

Annie hit the zoom. We worked within the truth of the pixels. I kept my eye on the tote cluster and counted. A round cat head, a little book, a tiny bell, a flag, a clean space big as a thumbprint with a faint rub mark and a tiny dangling back clasp, no front face. The star had left sometime before this minute.

The figure moves along our wall, one hand near the strap, the other pocketed. The height reads a hand shorter than me and a hand taller than Gran. The shoes carry no heel click. The watch strap shows for one frame when the wrist turns under the tote, thin leather, narrow keeper. We printed two stills. We did not write a name on a wrist. We wrote what we saw.

At 6:59:04, the figure stalls at our back door. The key strip I taped across the jamb after Asa sealed last night sits clean in the corner of the frame. The person stands inside the camera's window a full beat, then steps to the right where the awning keeps the drizzle from finding hair. The tote's pins catch the light twice more. The empty halo reads clear. The strap rides low. The person waits.

The router at 7:05 had seen a Chamber pool iPad join our Guest. I checked my watch and let the numbers settle. 7:05 aligns with the way a person who stands in our back pocket would wake a cached device that thinks our network is still its friend. The camera tells a story that matches the log. I like when the world refuses to contradict itself.

At 7:04:58, the figure checks the phone and glances down the alley. No one arrives. The tote shifts again, pins flash. The missing star reads like a tooth gap in a school photo. At 7:07:16 on their overlay, which is 7:06:16 for us, the figure steps into the open, crosses the alley slice, and leaves the frame. No face. No voice. A silhouette with a cluster that has one slot open.

"Export six forty-five to seven fifteen," I said.

Annie saved an MP4 to the sleeve we brought and burned two stills at 6:58:12 and 7:05:09 for the file. She printed her camera time with the offset note we gave her. She signed the envelope and let us sign with her. Chain lives in ink, not smiles. We thanked her with coffee later. For now, we walked back.

Asa met us in the hall. I set the envelope on the cart and wrote the transfer time. He opened it, skimmed the stills, and looked at me with that blank face he uses when he accepts a page as true and saves his opinion for the next step.

"No face," he said.

"No need yet," I said. "The tote reads louder than the head. Pins in a set, one slot empty."

"Show me your slot," he said, and did not flinch at his own sentence.

I set the still under the desk lamp. The gap sits top row, right side. The pin backs, two, anchor holes in the fabric, show bare, the rub line around them makes a faint circle. A small thread from the binding has pulled and rests on the rub. You only see it if you stare too long. I stare too long as a hobby.

"Now the ground," I said.

Back door, right side, where the figure stood to avoid the drip. The concrete holds dust and the kind of grit a lane carries when trucks roll. I got on my knees with a flashlight and a gloved hand and swept the space under the rack where we park boxed returns. Two book boxes stacked last night still sat. The broom missed the narrow slice under the lower crossbar. Pebbles, one paperclip, two lost buttons, a torn price sticker, a pin back clasp, and an enamel star face down in the dust, blue with a silver edge, no face check needed.

I did not touch it. I set the scale. Rafi took the photo. I slipped a thin spatula under the edge, lifted the star onto glass, and then into a sleeve. The clasp side showed a bent post and a smear of gray. The face had a micro nick at one point where enamel had chipped. The size fits the halo on the tote. The design matches Chamber giveaway pins from last quarter. We have three in a box from a pancake breakfast. I pulled that box and set one beside the new find under the phone scope. Enamel thickness matched, edge cut matched, back stamp matched. My hands wanted to draw the line with a marker. I used a pencil.

"Say it," Asa said.

"Title office camera shows a figure with a Chamber tote at 6:58 to 7:07," I said. "The tote's pin cluster carries an empty slot, halo ring shows where a star lived. We recovered an enamel star pin under our back rack, bent post, face down, consistent with Chamber pins. The timeline lands between the two moments the Chamber pool iPad touched our Guest at 5:58 and 7:05. A person stood where that pin fell."

He nodded and looked at the pin through the sleeve without touching it. He never touches. He looked at the still one more time. He put both in his notebook and clipped them with one of his clean clips like he was tacking a moth he did not plan to keep.

Gran arrived with the witness ledger and wrote the pin as recovered at 11:26 a.m., back rack, right of door, under crossbar. She drew a tiny star in the margin and smirked at herself once. I let her have it.

Peppermint came to the threshold and sat, eyes on the gap under the rack. He stuck his paw in, pulled out the paperclip, ignored the star. He batted the clip once, lost interest, and stared at the still. Cats like clusters. They pretend not to.

Rafi ran a quick batch on the star pin under the lamp. Enamel chips glitter in a boring way. The smear on the post smelled like concrete dust, not wax, not oil. The post had a fresh kink at the base, the kind you get when a pin snags and you pull without slowing down. The clasp we found three inches over looked torn at the spring side. This makes a pair. I slid both into one bag, wrote two entries on one card, and linked them in ink. If a person argues the star came from Christmas three years ago, the bent post and the torn clutch from last night win.

I pulled the Chamber's social feed while the room breathed. They had posted twice yesterday. A morning photo of Celeste in the hall with a board of donors, smiling, holding the tote we now had on stills. In that frame the tote carried five pins across the top seam. Cat, book, bell, flag, star. The star sat where our video shows the empty halo. The second post at 4:12 p.m. shows Celeste on our sidewalk under balloons, same tote, same five pins. The star sits in its slot, no chip. I printed both posts. I drew a circle around the star in each and wrote the times. The earlier post puts the star on the tote before the event. The still at 6:58 shows the gap. The floor gives us the star near our rack. I do not need a speech.

"Post them," I said to Rafi. "Sleeves, not a corkboard. No room for thumbtacks today."

He slipped both prints into sleeves and wrote the URL with a clean hand so a clerk who hates me can find the originals later. He pulled the EXIF where the feed allows it and wrote the time the Chamber uploaded. They will delete nothing until Asa prints their logs. Screenshots live in our folder too.

Asa rounded the back door and set his palm on the jamb near the seal. He reads rooms like a carpenter, not a poet. He lets his eye go to the ground then to the hand height then to the tote height, he marks points without the rest of us seeing his pencil move. When he looked back at me his face held a kind of settled focus that tells me he will carry this line to the meeting he has planned with the Chamber administrator at noon.

"Anyone else carry that tote with that cluster," he said.

"Other volunteers have the same tote and base set of pins," I said. "Cluster arrangement differs. The cat pin and the bell swap on some. The star sits left or right depending on who loaded their board. Celeste put her star far right. That matches the halo in the still. That matches the star under the rack. That matches the posts we printed. That is what I can say."

"What you can swear becomes what I want," he said.

"Then I will say it again for the recorder," I said.

He held up the small field recorder. I gave the same sentence in that flat, tidy way he likes, with times, with the offset note, with the seal that I will not sign the wrong word to learn a lesson. He clicked stop and put the thing in his bag.

Peppermint crept into the frame on the still, stared at the blank where the star should live, then blinked two slow blinks at the star in the sleeve. He wanted me to think he connected them. He likes keeping me humble.

I took one more look at the alley file. At 6:58 the figure arrives. At 7:05 the device associates with our Guest. At 7:07 the figure leaves. No one else in the frame during that window stops at our sill. No one else stands still enough to drop a pin and go fishing under a rack. Logs and glass tell the same story with two accents. Good.

Rafi pulled one more still at 7:00:41 when a gust lifts the tote front. You can see four pins clearly and that gap. He printed it, circled the gap, marked the time, and slid it next to the first two in one sleeve with a gray insert so the toner does not stick. He does this without needing praise. He holds his own standards.

Gran tapped the ledger and read her last line. "Star pin recovered under rack," she said. "Chamber posts show star present before event."

I opened the pancake breakfast box and held one of the spare star pins next to the recovered one. Same size. Same back stamp. Same enamel blend under our lamp. The recovered one had a chip at a point. The spare had no chip. I wrote chip at point on the card. Chips tell. They sit in pockets and scratch hands when a person pushes inside for a phone or a ticket. The person will remember later and lie without meaning to. The chip will not.

Asa asked one more question before heading to the Chamber office.

"Why would the star fall under the rack and not at the door," he said.

"Backpack strap and tote strap twist when a person stands and waits," I said. "Pins rub the seam and catch the crossbar lip. The spring clutch we found three inches over likely released when the person shifted and dragged the tote so the points scraped the iron. The bent post says pull, not a straight drop."

"Okay," he said. He does not feed a theory until it eats.

He left. Rafi carried the US drive to the safe. I printed the offset note and taped it to the envelope with the MP4. We documented the title office system time, our sync, and the correction so a person who tries to get clever with one minute will sit back down. I do not let small slippages ruin a day.

I stood at the back door and looked through the glass at the rack base. The alley read normal, a person with a tote had been normal too until normal refused to fit the time. I wrote a card for the file, placed it on the board above the audit strip from the till, and backed away.

6:58 to 7:07, figure with Chamber tote at our back door. Gap in pin cluster where star lives. Star recovered under back rack. Chamber posts show star present before event. Router logs support presence at 7:05. The line holds.

Peppermint flicked dust off his paw and went to his stool. He is done when I am done, not the other way round.

The room felt steadier. The pile of paper on the counter grew into a low wall between a story and the truth. If a person wants to climb it, they can, and I have a ladder with rungs named time, device, glass, and pin. I would rather they sit at the table and speak the words the room wants.

Before we closed the loop, I checked the Chamber feed again to be sure no one behind a desk had scrubbed, rotated, or played neat with history. Both posts still lived. Comments started to gather under the balloons photo. Prayers and frowns and one person who always finds a way to make a tragedy look like they need a new coat. I saved the feed to PDF in case someone decides to set their house on fire and call it a remodel.

Gran made tea and set a cup on a coaster, no ring in sight. Rafi cleaned the rack base because evidence had left and dust did not deserve to stay. I set the recovered star in the case folder, labeled it with a simple thing.

Back rack. 7:07 window. The missing point.

End of the hour, Asa texted a single screenshot from the Chamber's page, the morning post, Celeste's tote with the star on the far right where the halo lives in our still. He had circled it with a clean line. No emojis. No comment.

The star was present there.

CHAPTER 12

Gran Remembers

Gran's garage smells like oil, cedar, and old paper. The shelves run in clean rows, labeled in her hand. She does not hoard. She archives.

We parked Peppermint Cat business on the gravel and ducked under the pull cord. Gran flicked the chain on a clamp light and pointed to a banker's box with blue tape. Donations, Town Library, Special. She touched the lid like a notary.

"Asa wants chain," I said.

"He gets chain," she said.

Rafi rolled the cart in from the trunk with our flatbed scanner, sleeves, and the witness ledger. Asa stood near the workbench, notebook open, eyes steady. He keeps his hands still in other people's rooms.

Gran set the banker's box on the bench. She wrote the time in our ledger. 11:58 a.m., garage archive, donation ledger, registry card, restoration file. She underlined garage. She let the line sit.

Inside the box, folders sat edge out, labeled by year. She pulled one marked Restoration and another marked Ledger. She placed both on a clean blotter and opened the ledger first, a clothbound book with tabbed months and a line for each transfer.

She ran her finger down a page that has already lived two audits.

"Here," she said.

Entry: October 14, ten years back. Item: Town ex-libris stamp head and base. Outgoing, H&K Conservation. Courier: Quickstep. Waybill: QS-21173. Custodian signature: G. Wren. Witness signature: M. Foreman.

Next line. November 3, same year. Item: Town ex-libris stamp head and base. Incoming, H&K Conservation. Courier: Quickstep. Waybill: QS-22119. Condition notes: Face cleaned, ear tip dressed, minor ring nick at ten set by technician during correction. Custodian signature: G. Wren. Witness signature: M. Foreman.

She turned the page. December of that year shows Encasing Day. Base mounted to acrylic. Head pressed once for standard registry. Card filed. Photo filed. Seal applied. Keys cut, two, logged by number. Custodian and witness signed again.

I photographed each spread with the scale and today's paper in frame. Rafi scanned and saved PDFs to the case folder. Gran initialed the margin of each scan sheet. Asa read the lines as if they were numbers on a meter. No comment. He prefers the page to speak.

"Registry," I said.

Gran opened the Restoration folder and pulled a narrow envelope. Inside sat the cream registry card in a Mylar sleeve. She slid it out and placed it under the lamp. The blind impression rose under the light. Round border. Our cat. Library text. The ear tip showed a faint flat. The ring at ten showed a tiny set nick, deliberate, diagnostic. The date on the back of the card matched the ledger. The initials in the corner were hers and the foreman's.

She set a photo beside it. Monochrome print from the conservator's exit file. The die face under a raking light, ruler in frame, ear tip with the same flat, ring with the same nick. A technician had marked both on the print with a grease pencil. Their initials lived in the lower border with a ticket number. H&K liked tidy proof. So do I.

"Chain me through," Asa said.

Gran ran the short version like she was at a desk in the old building. "Stamp left on October fourteenth, ten years back. Returned November third with ear tip dressed and a small diagnostic nick at the ring near ten. We pressed the registry on Encasing Day, same winter, then sealed the case. Keys split. From that day the stamp logged in this book only for controlled tests. It never left again."

I set the registry card on the mat, placed our blind test scrap from the shop next to it, and brought the lamp low. The ear on the registry carried a flat you can feel with a fingernail. The ring at ten carried the nick the tech set when he corrected a burr. Our scrap carried neither. Ear point sharp. Ring clean.

Rafi photographed the pair wide and then close. He shot the ear and the ring in matched angles. He slid the images into sleeves and labeled them: Registry Ear. Shop Test Ear. Registry Ring Ten. Shop Test Ring Ten.

"Ledger entries after the seal," I said.

Gran flipped forward. Five controlled opens in ten years. One for a museum loan form that never left the room. Three for school days when she taught docents how to read paper without touching. One test last summer when I documented the base and adjusted the acrylic. Each line carries her name, a witness, the time the case opened, the time it closed, and a note that the head never left the room. No long gaps. No vague words. No missing signatures.

"Keys," Asa said.

Gran opened a small tin with two brass tags. One reads Cat Case 1. The other reads Cat Case 2. The second tag sits in a tiny envelope marked Chamber copy, surrendered and returned on Encasing Day. Return signature sits under it. Celeste's name does not appear anywhere near that line. She would not. She was not in office then.

I photographed the tag envelope and the return signature. I did not need to enjoy it to trust it.

Gran pulled a small manila pouch from the bottom of the box. "H&K packet," she said.

Inside, a copy of the conservator's report. Surface: grime removed, burr corrected. Note: diagnostic nick set at ring near ten to mark correction. Note: ear tip dressed, micro flat remains by design for track. Photo plates attached. Outbound and inbound waybills stapled. Box weight recorded to the gram. The signature of the receiving clerk at our old building sat under a stamp. Same date as the ledger.

Rafi scanned the report and the plates and saved them to the folder. He named them with the ticket number and the year so no one will lose them when they go hunting on a bad day. Asa read the plates and drew a short line under the diagnostic note in his book.

"From the return to Encasing Day, who had custody," he said.

"Me and the foreman," Gran said. "Two of us every time. No volunteers. No Chamber staff. The stamp sits in this line," she tapped the ledger, "until we sealed the case. After that, the head was never signed out by anyone but Liora this morning for the blind bite test under camera."

She looked at me without heat. She does not need to say take care. I do.

We laid the registry card, the H&K photo, and our scrap in a row and brought the lamp to the same side for each. Micro pitting on the registry and the H&K plate align like a star map. Our scrap's pit pattern veers in three zones. The ear flat shows on the registry and plate. Our scrap shows none. The ring nick at ten lives on the registry and the plate. Our scrap shows none.

"Say it," Asa said, clean.

"Chain shows the stamp left on October fourteenth, returned November third with a diagnostic nick at ten and a flat on the ear tip," I said. "We pressed a registry under controlled weight and sealed the case. The ledger shows no departures. The registry and the conservator's photo agree. The object under our acrylic does not."

Gran put a hand on the ledger, then on the registry card. She does not grandstand. She anchors.

"You can print that," she said to Asa. "I will sign it again."

He nodded once. He did not make a speech. He took a still of the row with his phone and texted it to himself with a label only he would use.

Rafi scanned the ledger pages that matter and printed a small packet to hand across the table. He put the registry photo and the H&K plate behind a sheet of acetate so the toner would not transfer. He wrote a cover sheet. Town Ex-libris, chain and registry, Gran Wren, custodian.

Gran closed the ledger, then opened a second box without being asked. She held up a sponsor card from six winters back with a stamp impression we made at a docent day with the real head before we sealed it again. Blind impression under the same lamp. Ear flat. Ring nick at ten. A second confirmation from a day when no one breathed hard. We photographed that too and slipped it behind the packet.

"Why keep that one," I asked.

"Because people forget," she said.

Outside, a car door thumped. Inside, the clamp light hummed. Gran's garage made its usual quiet space for truth.

Peppermint is never in the garage, which keeps the paper safe. I still wrote his name in the witness ledger because it makes me smile when I read the list of people who hold this place to a standard. Gran gave me a look that says do not get cute. I crossed it out. She nodded. It is our dance.

Asa asked one more question for his record. "Any loan after Encasing Day," he said.

"No," Gran said. "Not to the Chamber. Not to the school. Not to the county. People asked. We showed them the registry and the photo and told them the stamp had retired."

"Anyone at the Chamber sign this ledger," he said.

"No," she said. "They do not sign my books."

He wrote both answers and left the page open for her to see. He does that when he wants the room to feel like a partner, not a drawer.

Rafi sealed the packet in a sleeve and labeled it for transfer. Asa signed the chain card. Gran signed as custodian. I signed as the clerk who has to sleep with this shop's keys in her pocket. We do these things because bad days do not forgive sloppy hands.

We packed the box like we found it, with the ledger on top so Gran can reach it without standing on a stool. She slid the banker's box back to its spot and ran her palm along the blue tape like a person patting a child's shoulder at a crosswalk.

I looked at the registry photo one more time before the sleeve closed. The nick at ten is small. You would not see it if you did not know where to look. You know where to look because someone ten years back cut it on purpose to keep future clerks honest. That is why I love that kind of shop.

We drove back with the packet flat on the back seat. Rafi held a hand on it when we hit a pothole. Habit. The office felt brighter when we laid the packet next to the binder. The lamp ate the shadows and threw the nick into view. The thing under our acrylic threw nothing but a clean ring and a sharp ear.

I unlocked the vitrine with the same key I dusted, lifted the acrylic two inches so the light would not glare, and stared at the face. No flat on the ear. No nick at ten. The pitting map crooked. The polish striations we saw earlier again catching light. The registry card on the desk said no. The photo from H&K said no. The ledger said no. Gran's docent card from six winters back said no.

I lowered the acrylic and locked it. I held the key where the camera could see it and dropped it back in the cup. Gran wrote the time in the lock log. Asa looked at the seal and at me. He waits for the words because words carry weight when you keep them small.

"Swap confirmed," I said.

CHAPTER 13

Alternate Heat

A room gets loud when people think guilt hunts the noisiest throat. I do not hunt by volume. I sort by time.

We started on the shop floor where the bay brace caught light and the cones did their quiet job. The tent on Oak still stood from last night. Banners down. Tables stacked. A few volunteers wandered with clipboards like strays after a parade. I set my binder on the counter and wrote the line that would hold the morning.

Clear the loud. Log the minute.

Gran opened the witness ledger and wrote 12:42 p.m., alternate suspect grid, shop floor and tent. Rafi stood by the screen with the camera feeds queued. Asa took the end of the counter where he could look at a door and a page at the same time. Peppermint stretched once, then settled with his chin on the register rail. Texture, not help.

Four names had drawn heat because heat likes a target. Nina with her sharpened tongue. Bria with her booth hustle. Harold with his big pocket and bigger opinions. Paula because people confuse presence with motive. All four had motions last night. Not one had room to swing a press.

"Run Nina," Asa said.

Nina works our town like a whetstone. She scrapes against any plan until sparks jump. Yesterday she argued with Celeste at four and again at five forty. She did not like the Chamber's sponsorship board or the optics of the tote. She liked the Founders Ledger too much. She had walked back and forth in front of our bay like a metronome. Ten people could remember her voice. That makes her a magnet, not a murderer.

Rafi pulled the indoor clip from 6:15 to 6:25. At 6:18:12 Nina stood at the tent mic under the front awning with the raffle jar. The time burned in the lower corner. The tent camera runs on our system. We had the feed and the file. She read three names and then argued lightly with Harold about whether matching pledges should trigger another round. The crowd laughed. She rolled her eyes and read a fourth name. At 6:19:03 you can see heads turn toward the alley as the back chime sounds in the shop. Nina keeps reading. At 6:20:08 she pings the jar with a spoon. The sound lands on the recording like a bell. At 6:21:02 the mic picks up a small hush and one sharp intake near the door as the press hits the hall. Nina says keep the lane clear, please, and sets the jar down. Her mouth moves on script. Her feet stay planted on a taped X a foot behind the table.

"Angle two," I said.

The front overhang cam shows the awning edge and the mic stand from the side. At 6:18 the mic stand shadow sits behind Nina's skirt hem. At 6:19 the shadow has not shifted. At 6:20 she touches the jar. At 6:21 she raises her hand to her brow and looks toward the shop door. She does not run. She does not exit the frame. She stays on the taped X until I step to the doorway at 6:21:18 and call time. She is not in our hall. She is not near the ladder or the press.

"Audio pulls her off the board," Asa said.

"Yes," I said. "Mic proves her mouth and body at the tent during the chime and the fall. She had range to throw a look. No range to swing iron."

Gran wrote the sentence without embroidery. Nina on mic 6:18 to 6:21, tent feed, no hall access.

"Run Bria," Asa said.

Bria ran the vendor line and the booth cash, which means she ran. She carried a waist pouch, a square reader, a clean pencil, and a list that would break a lesser spine. People who do five things at once draw suspicion because their hands touch many tables. Hands with receipts are a gift.

Rafi pulled the tent vendor cam from 6:16 to 6:24. At 6:17:40 Bria stands at Table B with a buyer trying to pay cash with damp bills. She smiles and points at the donation jar and takes card instead. At 6:18:12 she slides to Table D and runs a card for ten. The Square terminal logs the time. We pulled the batch this morning. Rafi projected the transaction ID on the screen with 18:18:13. She jogs to the espresso island at 6:19:09 for a stack of tasting cups, grabs them, and heads back to Table C without passing the hall. At 6:20:21 she swipes for twenty on the same terminal. The log reads it. At 6:21:05 she leans across a display to catch a falling bookmark. The camera freezes people in the doorway. Bria is in frame, shoulder deep in a booth.

I pulled her Square batch on paper and laid the strip under the still. 18:18:13 sale complete. 18:20:21 sale complete. Both show the last four digits of a local card we can call if we want a voice later. I do not need it. The timer and the frame hold.

"Phone location," I said.

Bria handed over her phone without drama because she trusts our shop and hates rumors. We opened the photo roll and found two Live Photos she took for social scrub. The first at 18:18:16 of a reader card she wanted to remember. The second at 18:20:24 of a cat sticker display. Metadata sets both within ten feet of the tent terminal. Live Photos carry two seconds of sound. In the first you can hear Nina read a raffle name. In the second you can hear the spoon ping the jar at 6:20. She is not a footstep from the hall. She is in the tent.

"Say it," Gran said.

"Bria's Square log and her phone place her at tent tables at 6:18 and 6:20. The aisle microphone draws the sound she heard. At 6:21 the booth cam shows her inside the tent line, not in the hall. She was not near the ladder or the press."

Asa nodded. He does not give out praise for clearing the obvious. He saves it for the step where someone tries to force blame onto a body that does not fit. I am not there yet.

"Run Harold," he said.

Harold pledges in public with a voice like an auctioneer. He likes being seen holding a check. He likes sliding his wallet out with a flourish. He matched a pledge at 6:19, he said later, with a number twice what the jar needed. Heat finds money and makes it look like guilt. We count instead.

Rafi printed the till rollback strip again so I could line it above the tent feed. At 6:19 on the tent audio you can hear Harold clap and say double it, I will match that, now you read mine. At 6:19:28 he claps again. The camera shows his back at the donation table under the awning, shoulder to shoulder with a woman in a green jacket, the one who runs the food pantry. Her face sits on the frame, mouth open with laughter. She holds a matching slip and a flat of brownies. At 6:19:52 Harold raises his arm with a check. He does not move toward the hall. At 6:20:11 he leans across to sign the pledge board while Nina hits the jar with the spoon. He fits inside that circle. He does not exit it.

I ran his check through the camera with a zoom. Bank name. Routing masked by his thumb. Amount. We will not speak it here. His dress shoes sit on two strips of gaffer tape I set the day before to keep the table from shuffling. Those strips make a neat alibi. The tape does not move until 6:24 when chairs scrape and the crowd breaks. He could not have walked down the hall in time to swing and get back on his mark while still holding a line about generosity. He is not that fast.

"Paula," Asa said.

Paula is a station unto herself in any room. She moved people like water around a rock, calm and stern and right. People watch the current and think the rock controls the river. She controlled nothing but time and small kindness. That still draws eyes.

Rafi pulled the bay angle and the counter angle from 6:15 to 6:22. At 6:15 she slides the guestbook under the stand on Celeste's cue for "flow." At 6:16 she draws a map line on the floor with her hand and points a frail donor toward the chairs, then returns to the bay. At 6:18 she is three feet inside the door with one hand on a cone and the other on a child's shoulder, gently turning the body away from the brace line. At 6:19, the chime sounds. Paula looks toward the back and tells the child a small joke about cones being traffic hats. The child smiles and starts a whisper. At 6:20 she watches the tent when the spoon pings. At 6:21, when I call time, she points at the floor and says stay here, and she stays. The frame for the hall shows my back, not Paula's. The frame for the bay shows her hand on the cone and her feet inside the tape.

I pulled the espresso till audit one more time for context. RBK and VOID land at 6:11 and 6:12. Not her. Sponsor card ghosts belong to the Chamber glass. Not her. The scrape on the track sits at 32 inches. She does not carry a lanyard with a spring gate. She carries a blunt key on a cloth loop we made at Blind Date Night last year.

Gran wrote a line that could live on a board in a school. Presence is not proximity. Proximity is not action. At 6:19 through 6:21 Paula stands at the bay.

I looked up and let the room settle. I took Nina off the board first because the mic made it easy. I took Bria off next because the Square printout is my favorite kind of alibi. I took Harold off because tape on the ground and a loud promise keep a person planted. I took Paula off because the camera refuses to lie.

"Say the minutes back to me," Asa said.

"Chime at 6:19. Press fall at 6:21," I said. "Nina on mic 6:18 to

6:21. Bria on Square at 6:18 and 6:20, in frame at 6:21. Harold at the pledge table at 6:19 and 6:20. Paula at the bay from 6:15 through the call at 6:21. None near the ladder. None in the back hall. None near the press. Each tied to a clock or a cam."

Gran underlined each time in the ledger. She does not draw arrows. She draws small dots that turn into anchors in a reader's eye.

"Bring me their voices anyway," Asa said.

We did, one by one, not as suspects, as clocks.

Nina stood at the counter with her hair pinned back and a look that says she has sharpened thoughts and knows when to sheathe them. She watched the still where her own mouth forms the name that came up in the raffle. She listened to the ping on the jar. She played the clip of silence when the press hit and kept her face still.

"I said keep the lane clear," she said. "I said it because people panic toward noise. I did not know what fell. If you need my shoes, take them. They never left that mark."

"We have you on the feed," I said. "We need your temper later, not your shoes."

She snorted, which is a compliment in Nina's language.

Bria brought her Square batch on her own printout and a photo of the table map with time stamps in the corners. She hates sloppy shop talk and proved her clean with receipts. She asked me if we wanted the steps from her phone. I said no. The terminal logs lived enough for me.

"I did not hear the press," she said. "I felt the crowd pull and held the table because I know what chaos does to shelves."

"You did good," I said.

She gave a short nod and went back to helping Rafi coil the tent string because Bria is never idle.

Harold arrived with a folded copy of his check and a second pledge sheet in case the town wanted to act big in public again.

He likes being useful. He likes being seen being useful. That sits fine with me when numbers need a spine.

"I stood here and here," he said, pointing at the tape. "If the tape is true, then I stayed."

"The tape is true," I said.

He breathed out, shoulders lower by an inch. He asked if we wanted pastries for the crew. I said yes because saying no to pastry is foolish.

Paula closed the bulletin and stepped over with her own map in her head. She watched the frame of herself turning the child, then the frame where she touches the cone at the call. She smiled at the child again in memory.

"I have nothing to add," she said. "Except that when people panic, they forget cones save ankles."

"Write that on your board," I said.

"I did," she said, and she had.

We let the room breathe. People who like noise ran out of names in the first round and will need new toys. I will not give them any. We had other lines to follow.

I stood at the rare nook and looked at the ladder scar again. Gray bloom on one foot. Clean on the other. The swing wrote the same arc as the dust swipe on the shelf. That is the hand we keep chasing. It is quieter than Nina's temper, faster than Bria's pace, softer than Harold's pledge, calmer than Paula's station. Quieter does not mean clean.

Rafi printed a one-page grid with four bars for 6:18 to 6:22. He colored each with a pencil he reserves for maps. Nina: tent mic. Bria: tent Square. Harold: pledge table. Paula: bay cones. He placed the grid next to the audit strip for RBK and VOID at 6:11 and 6:12. He added a small star sticker on 6:19 for the chime. He added a small ladder doodle at 6:21 for the fall. He is not an artist. He is clear.

Gran wrote a line at the bottom of the ledger page. Loud is not guilty. Time is.

Asa closed his notebook and looked toward the back hall like a person listening for a shift in an old house. He has a carpenter's ear. He does not love chalkboards. He loves weight.

"Now who had room to work," he said.

"Celeste," I said. "At 6:12 with the reprint. At 6:15 with the guestbook move. At 6:19 near the hall. At 6:21 not on any mic. The router saw a Chamber iPad at 5:58 and again at 7:05."

He nodded once. He did not smile. He saved his battery for the next knock on a door that wears a seal.

We walked the tent line one more time to be fair. I checked the vendor pole for marks. None. I checked the alley mouth for a slip that could explain a run. None. I checked the floor wax at the tent's edge. All citrus lived inside the shop, not here. The air smelled like card stock and cold coffee and city dust. It did not smell like need.

Rafi tugged the tent edge free and rolled the fabric tight. He taped the roll with two clean bands, wrote the time, and stacked it along the wall. He cleans our day with the same care I clean a page. It keeps us from slipping on our own tools.

Peppermint dozed through the role call and woke when the copier spit a test page at noon. He is a clerk in his head. He believes the day should end with a stack of paper and a nap on a warm chair.

Asa's phone buzzed with a patrol text. The Chamber's admin had printed pool device sign-outs and a lanyard box count. One pool iPad lacked a current signature. The box count was two short of a bundle. The star pins in their supply did not match the chip on ours. He sent a photo of the missing slot on their tote board with a little square of tape where a star should hang. He wrote bring your file in the reply to his own phone so he will not forget to ask for signatures with times.

We gathered on the floor around the counter and looked up at the board. The day had rules now. We let them settle and hold.

At 12:58 the router page on the office screen ticked a tiny line. Rafi saw it first because he always does. A client name blinked on the Guest list for a breath.

CR-iPad, associate 19:05 yesterday. Cached captive portal. Remembered client.

No new association now. The line came from the log scrolling in review. He froze the page and magnified the last seen field. We had seen it before. We had written it. He flagged it with a yellow box and looked at me.

"Seven oh five," he said.

"Someone stayed," I said.

The room held that line like a weight set on the table. It made the coffee cups shift a hair. It made the pencil roll a little. It made my hand want to move the case file one inch to the right.

Gran wrote the words on the ledger under the grid of names. Seven oh five. Someone stayed.

CHAPTER 14

Hardware Truth

The back room bench holds what people pretend they do not see. Metal. Dust. Threads that tell on hands.

Rafi rolled the press plate onto the padded horses and set the base on the bench with the feet toward us. Asa stood in the doorway so his shadow lived on the floor where the camera could read it. Gran opened the witness ledger and wrote the time. 1:28 p.m., press base inspection, screws and shelf lip. She underscored the word screws once.

"Clean light," I said.

Rafi clipped the two task lamps to the shelf and raked them low. Iron learns your eye if you give it the right angle.

The base holds four carriage screws through the plate into the foot blocks. Three wore age the way good boots do. Heads dull, slots grayed, edges rounded from decades of being left alone. One did not belong. Front right. Zinc bright. Slot edges crisp. Washer clean as a coin no one has touched until last night.

Gran leaned closer without crossing the tape. "Say the difference," she said.

"Three original, blacked steel with varnish haze and packed dust at the head," I said. "One replacement, zinc plated, no varnish haze, sharp slot. Washer shows a fresh burnish ring."

Rafi passed me the loupe. I set it to the new head. The slot walls looked cut this week, not this decade. The burr along the slot's inner face still threw a glitter. The washer below held a bright crescent where a driver shank would rub if a hand missed the slot on the first try. Across the plate, an old head sat in its crust like a fossil. No glitter. No fresh crescent.

"Threads," I said.

He flipped the base and braced it so the feet pointed up. We keep a thin wire brush for this. I blew, Rafi brushed, and the hole for the new screw showed a cord of clean spiral, a bright, fresh bite. The holes for the three old screws still wore brown dust in their grooves. Packed. Familiar. The kind of grip a thread gets when wood and iron have slept together for half a century.

Asa moved one step in. "Photograph," he said.

Rafi shot the new hole first, scale card on the edge. Clean spiral. Bright. Then he shot the old holes. Dust in the grooves. Then the underside of the plate where sawdust compacts and lives. He took a close of the new washer ring and the tiny burr at the slot. He took the full base for context.

I ran a cotton swab along the inner edge of the new slot and bagged the trace. Slight gray. Slight oil. No flavor of our floor wax. Iron from the head and a smear of human skin oil from whoever drove it. Lab can make it louder later. Today the shine reads enough.

"Count shavings," I said.

Rafi held a magnet under the foot block and drew a faint fan of bright specks, the kind you get when a driver kisses a slot and scrapes. He tapped the specks into a fold of paper and slid them into a coin envelope. On the bench, under the new head, a single tiny curl of zinc sat where a person took one scrape too hard before the slot settled. He slid that into the same envelope and labeled it. Zinc curl from new head. Specks from foot block under new head.

"Old screws," I said.

We chose the least stubborn of the old heads and tried a quarter turn with a proper flat driver. The head refused to budge. The driver flatted in the groove without travel. You do not force a relic. We put it back the way we found it. The point was not to move anything. The point was to read what had moved.

I put the loupe to the underside of the shelf lip above the press slot, a place where a hand would brace and where a tool slips when someone works fast. A small skitter line ran at an angle. Same place I clocked a nick when we stood here first thing. Fresh wood bright, not aged. Next to it, a deeper ding with two parallel striations that make a signature. Not crosscut. Not a nail. The kind of mark a driver shaft leaves when it jerks and bites.

"Scale," I said.

Rafi took the macro. The striations ran five millimeters apart, shallow. He put a metric strip in the frame. He took a second photo from the other lamp so we could see grain. I tapped the lip with my knuckle. The wood gave that thin note a shelf gives when a tool has scraped it and the fibers are raw.

"Say it," Asa said.

"One base screw is new," I said. "Threads show a fresh bite. The other three are old and tight with packed dust. Washer under the new head carries a bright rub. Slot burr throws glitter. Shelf lip above holds a tool mark with a pair of striations that reads driver shaft slip."

Gran wrote the sentence. She does not like to waste ink. She wrote the word new with her square hand and underlined it.

Rafi checked the head size with a gauge. The slot measured for a 5.5 millimeter flat. The striation gap on the lip matched the shank diameter of a small driver we hand out at workshop nights when we fix loose chair screws and clock backs. Those free drivers live in totes.

"Which driver," Asa said.

"The tiny ones with the clear handles," I said. "Chamber swag last month included one with their logo. They set out a bowl beside the candy dish."

Gran nodded. She had one in her knitting bag for a week until she got sick of poking her finger on it.

"Check our lost and found," I said.

Rafi went to the back closet and pulled the plastic bin where abandoned giveaways live. Buttons, pens, ribbons, two keychains, a folded tote that had once held Chamber pamphlets, and a small screwdriver with a clear handle and a blue cap. The handle carried the Chamber logo and the word Together in tiny print. Bit size looked right. He slid it into a sleeve without touching the metal and wrote Lost and found, back closet, clear driver, Chamber logo.

"Hold," I said. "Not the end of it."

We still had the tote from last month's Chamber meeting stacked with other unclaimed swag. It sat on the high hook by the office, labeled with a sticky because I like sticks more than guilt trips. I lowered it and set it on the bench. Peppermint came to sniff the canvas and sat, bored, when it had no food scent. I tipped the tote and shook. Pens, a brochure, a pack of napkins, two lanyards without badges, a ball of string, and a small plastic pouch like the kind hardware stores use for bits.

The pouch held a stubby flat driver with a short shaft and a fat clear handle. Also a fold card that read Fix Your Space and a tiny zip bag with a second bit you can swap into the same handle. The flat bit measured with the gauge at 5.5. The tip had a bright polish on one wing and a micro chip on the other. The shank showed two faint scuff lines at five millimeters apart where it had rubbed wood or plastic and turned under load.

I did not cheer. I did not joke. I set it on the glass tile and took the photo with the striation gap on the shelf lip in frame. The shank carried the same two-line spacing we shot under the lip. I held the handle over the new head without touching. The bit and the slot looked cut for each other.

"Bag it," Asa said.

Rafi slid the driver and the bit pouch into a large sleeve, wrote Chamber swag tote, last month, staff hook, and initialed it. He shot the label before sealing. I wrote a card for the folder. Small driver from Chamber tote, flat 5.5, shank scuff twin to shelf lip striations.

"Who signed for the tote," Asa said.

"No one," I said. "They left it after the meeting with a note that said Take One on their table. We boxed the extras. We put the tote on the hook because the pens roll into the wrong places if you leave them in a pile."

"Who would have known where we hung it," he said.

"Staff who clean," I said. "Volunteers who help fold after events. Celeste stood under it when she posted a thank-you photo last month. She panned and the hook with the tote lived in the back of her frame. Anyone who watches her feed and wanted free tools saw it."

Gran lifted the registry card from Chapter 12 out of the packet and placed it next to the driver in a way that felt like she was setting two coins next to each other. I knew the mood. When you stack proof, small things grow teeth.

"Check driver tip under scope," Rafi said.

We set the clear-handled driver under the phone microscope and rolled the focus. The tip edge on the left wing had a tiny crush where it met a metal slot and twisted harder than a polite hand would twist. The right wing carried fine parallel grind marks from the factory, new. The left wing showed fresh smearing. We took that still. We set the new screw head under the same scope. The slot wall on the left shoulder held a fine smear that matched the driver wing. I am not a lab. I know a smear when I see one.

I ran a cotton swab along the driver shank at the spot where the scuff lines lived and bagged it. Tiny wood dust stuck. We have shelf dust from last night under a seal. The lab can match species later if the universe is kind. Today my nose told me pine dust, which fits our shelf.

"Old screws," Gran said, pointing again. "Someone loosened more than one or only the one."

"We will not back them out to learn which," I said. "We already see enough. One fresh bite. Three old and tight. That tells a sequence."

Asa ran his finger in the air near the base, not touching, drawing the arc of a hand. "Unseat one to let the base pivot," he said. "Leave the rest to look like age. Reach up and use the lip for balance. Miss the slot, hit the lip, scrape. Driver goes back in a tote. Nobody owns a tote because everyone owns a tote."

Rafi nodded. He likes when tools preach.

I lifted the press base and took a photo of the foot that wore wax yesterday. Left front. The swing pivots from that foot toward the hall. The new screw sits on the opposite front, right. Loosen the right, the base lifts there first, the left foot becomes the pivot, the swing arcs toward the door. That fits the smear we matched in Chapter 6 and the fall we logged in Chapter 3. Not poetry. Geometry.

"Say it clean," Asa said.

"New screw at front right," I said. "Fresh threads. Fresh burr. The shelf lip above shows a driver scrape. A small driver with the Chamber logo from last month's tote sits on our hook. Its shank scuff lines match the striation gap on the lip. Its tip bears a fresh smear consistent with the slot. The base would pivot around the left front foot if the right front backed off. That pivot fits the wax transfer on the left foot and the swing path toward the door."

Gran wrote each clause like a list. She likes lists when a day tries to drown.

"Check the tote for fibers," Asa said.

I held the tote over clean paper and tapped the seams with a gloved finger. One red nylon sliver fell and clung to the page. Rafi slid it into a sleeve. We have red from Chapter 8 on the rug and on the sill. The Chamber's lanyards shed like party favors. The tote had lived under them last month and last night. Fiber on the tote is only a chorus, not a solo. I did not sing about it. I wrote it down.

"Who handled the tote since the meeting," Asa said.

"Me," I said. "Rafi. Gran. Paula put it on the hook. No one else should have."

He wrote those names. He will verify with the camera that lives too wide and too honest for any of us to enjoy later.

We brought out the small driver from lost and found too. Clear handle, blue cap, logo. This one had a Phillips bit, not a flat. The bit did not match our head. Good to compare. The shank striation gap was narrower. It did not line with the lip signature. We bagged it anyway in case someone wants to argue we pulled the wrong tool from the wrong bin. The right tool sits in the Chamber tote. The wrong tool sits in our lost box. Both carry their own little truths. Only one fits.

Peppermint walked along the bench and set his chin on the tote's edge. He stared at the driver as if it might roll, then watched the shelf lip like it was a fish tank. He appreciates straight lines and straight screws. He does not admit it.

"Pull the Chamber meeting clip," I said.

Rafi queued up last month's after-hours feed. The Chamber set up a table by the back room with swag. Celeste on the clip with that smile teams learn from her. She held a tote and handed out pins with a proud angle in her wrist. On the table, a bowl of clear-handled drivers. She tapped the bowl with two fingers and said, you never know when a loose screw will spoil a photo. She liked her own lines. I remember because I was tired and it made me want water.

Asa watched that clip without comment. He cut a still and printed it. Celeste's hand, the bowl, the handles shining like candy. He slid the still into a sleeve behind the driver photo and wrote Last month, Chamber swag, drivers on table.

"Inventory at their office," he said.

"Ask for their reorder," I said. "Ask how many drivers they

ordered, how many left, and who signed the invoice. Ask if they restocked the bowl last week. Ask where the empties went."

He nodded. He will do that without me and then tell me the line that matters later.

Rafi printed the current layout for the bench. New screw head macro with burr. Washer burnish. Fresh thread hole. Old thread holes with dust. Shelf lip striations. Driver shank scuff lines. Driver tip smear. He printed the tote photo with the driver on the glass tile. He printed the swag clip still. He wrote small captions with times and places. He made my wall neat.

I wrote the card that will live next to the audit strip and the ring overlay and the router page. Press base shows one replaced screw with bright head and fresh thread bite. Shelf lip carries a driver scrape. Chamber swag tote on our hook holds a small flat driver whose shank marks match the lip and whose tip smear matches the slot. Pivot point lines with wax transfer and swing.

Gran closed the witness ledger and rested her palm on it for a beat. She looked at me with her teaching face. That face still knows how to set a class in order.

"Explain this to a person who does not understand tools," she said.

"Someone loosened one foot of the press to let it tip easier," I said. "They used a small screwdriver. They missed once and scraped our shelf. They left a fresh screw in the hole they worked. They put the screwdriver back in a tote with free stuff. We still have the tote."

"Good," she said, and signed the page.

Asa looked at the driver in the sleeve and then at the base. He has the same relationship with tools I have with paper. If you ask them clean, they answer. He nodded at the base once and at the sleeve once and then at me. He will carry this piece to the Chamber meeting like a brick.

"Anything else," he said.

"One more small thing," I said.

He waited.

I stepped to the shelf above the press where the dust arc we logged in Chapter 6 still showed its pale smile. I brought the lamp low and raked it again. A faint scratch sat at the end of the arc at the very edge near the door. Not the driver scrape. A tiny point press, then a skid line, then nothing. I put the scale down and shot it. If a pin on a tote scraped there as a strap swung while someone leaned in with the driver, it would leave that. The star we found under the back rack had a chipped point. If the tote came near this shelf while a hand worked the screw, a point could have kissed the lip here and dropped later by the door. It is a thin line. It sits in the folder with the same weight as any thin line. It earns its place by the company it keeps.

"File it," Asa said. "Do not marry it."

"I do not plan to," I said.

Rafi finished the photo run and packed the driver sleeve into the evidence box with a divider so it would not clack against the star pin sleeve. He logged the box number and set it in the safe. He wrote the time on the safe log. He smiles when a log looks like a square.

Peppermint found a warm patch on the bench paper and curled until his nose touched his tail. He does not care about screws. He cares about sun. Texture, not help.

I wiped the bench where swarf had fallen and taped the zinc curl envelope to the page with the macro photographs. That curl will mean more later when a person tries to claim they only touched the press to dust it. Dusters do not make zinc curls. Drivers do.

We locked the back room and walked to the counter. The wall of paper had grown. Router lines. Till strip. Ring overlay. Rug fibers. Key bow and spine line. Alley still with the gap where the star should be. Now the new head and the driver shank mark. The room did not feel louder. It felt heavier. That is how truth does its job.

Asa checked his watch. He had a meeting with the Chamber

administrator at two. He took copies of the driver photos, the swag still, and the base macro. He did not take the driver. He prefers to show pictures first and see how faces move.

"Do not touch that tote," he said.

"We will not," I said.

He left with a nod and a page that reads like a map.

Gran poured tea and set it on a coaster. No ring ghosts on our glass. Rafi labeled the bench photos with a small pencil he keeps behind his ear. I wrote one more card for the case file, the line that will carry from this bench to the next room where a question waits.

The press was loosened.

I put the card in the binder and closed the rings. The sound felt good.

Then I went to the staff hook, lifted the Chamber tote again, and thumbed the inner pocket where pamphlets hide. A folded flyer slid out. On the back, a tiny checklist in Celeste's hand. Pins. Cards. Drivers. Photo. She liked lists too. She carried a list that told on her without trying.

I bagged the flyer, wrote the time, and looked up. Rafi raised his eyebrows. Gran did not. She had already written the sentence I would say.

We found a matching small driver in the Chamber swag tote from last month's meeting.

CHAPTER 15

Stamp Test Live

If people want theater, give them a clean stage with rules. The counter does that better than any podium.

Gran stood to my left with the witness ledger open and her square pen ready. Asa took the corner where the front camera owns his face and not his hands. Rafi set the task lamp low and steady. Paula drifted in with a schoolteacher's quiet and took the nearest chair. Two regulars stayed back of the cones because they know the shop. Peppermint took the register stool and stared at the ink pad like it might purr.

"Read the line," Asa said.

Gran wrote and read. "Counter demonstration at 2:11 p.m. One live impression. Witnesses present. Purpose: compare alignment to registry photo and document with today's paper."

I held the key where both cameras could see it and unlocked the vitrine. The barium dust still ghosted the bow. I lifted the stamp head on a folded towel. Rafi filmed the carry to the counter and set the lamp so the die face caught a shallow rake. The ear tip glinted clean. No flat. The ring at ten held no nick. We all saw it. We did not say it yet.

"Pad," I said.

Rafi placed the archival pigment pad on the mat. Black. Slow dry.

It sits on paper like a dark thought and does not bleed. I checked the pad with the loupe for fibers and grit. Clean. I set three cream cards in a row and taped today's Gazette above them with the date loud in frame. Paula gave a small nod at that. She likes proof with a calendar on it.

"Registry photo," I said.

Gran laid the conservator's exit photo beside the cards and set the transparent overlay with the registration holes on pins. The overlay ring and ear live where they have lived for ten years. I do not call that nostalgia. I call it control.

"One impression," Asa said.

"One," I said.

I kissed the die to the pad with a light rock to wake the face. I pressed the face to the first card with a flat palm and counted five. No twist. No show. I lifted straight up and parked the head on the towel. The room breathed once.

The image sat dense and honest. Round border. Our cat. Library text. The ear tip printed sharp. The outer ring went slightly heavy at eight and shy at two. A drift you can feel in your thumb before your eye clocks it. I brought the overlay down and set the pins. The registry ring rode outside our fresh ring from ten to two by half a hair. From four to eight our fresh ring stepped wide. The ear on the overlay showed the tiny flat from the restoration. Our ear did not.

"Photograph," I said.

Rafi took frames wide, mid, and macro with the overlay anchored. He raked the lamp to throw tiny shadows in the valleys the face pressed. He shot the ear and the ring at ten and a control at four. He kept the Gazette masthead in the wide frame so no one with a robe and patience could claim these images came from last winter.

"Micro pits," I said.

I set the loupe on the cat's cheek and the inner ring. Ink fills valleys and prints them as specks inside the shape. The registry photo shows a steady constellation near the cheek, three dots in a slope. Our impression shows two and a faint tail, the same mismatch I logged blind under the lamp in Chapter 7. Along the inner ring at five the registry shows a neat string. Our string breaks, then resumes a degree later. A skip you cannot polish away. It is a map. It is not ours.

"Say it," Asa said.

"Live impression drifts off registry by roughly half a hair on the outer ring," I said. "Ear prints sharp, not flat. Micro pitting prints as a different pattern in three zones. Registry constellation at cheek shows three. Ours shows two and a ghost. Registry string at five prints continuous. Ours breaks and restarts."

Gran wrote it, small and calm. Paula watched the overlay and then watched the card again like a student who has already learned the answer and wants to see the work. The regulars stayed quiet. They know when to be furniture.

I slid the second card under the face and touched the pad again, this time with a lighter kiss to rule out an over-ink false tell. Same drift. Same ear. Same little betrayal in the pits. We do not hang all weight on one strike. Two gives the pattern a back.

Rafi shot both. He set the two cards beside the registry photo with the Gazette headline in frame. He printed a contact sheet on the back printer so Asa could walk with paper if he needed to.

Peppermint leaned forward until his nose hovered a whisker above the pad, sniffed with the insulted look he keeps for citrus and lavender, then splayed his toes and stared at the die like it owed him rent. Texture. Not help.

"Document it," Gran said.

I wrote the line on the case card with my square hand so my future self would not curse me. 2:13 p.m., live impression under witnesses. Overlay drift half hair. Ear prints without restoration flat. Micro pitting diverges at cheek, inner ring five. Photographed with Gazette date.

Asa looked at the cards and did not smile. He smiled earlier when the driver mark met the shelf lip. He does not smile for this. He signed the witness line in the ledger. Paula initialed under his name with that tidy teacher signature. Rafi stamped the image numbers in the margin of the binder like a person who will sleep well.

I lifted the head to clean the face. You do not scrub. You breathe and touch the edge of a lintless cloth and coax the pigment out of valleys. The face will keep ink in pitted spots, which is a gift today. Rafi took one macro of the wet pits for the folder. You can see the void where the registry carries a dot. You can see the dot where ours carries a void. That is not poetry. That is a record.

"Base," I said.

The head sits on a wooden base block with a pad between iron and wood. Ours looked newer than I like. The weave had that fresh polyurethane sheen you get from a modern gasket sheet. Gran's face told me she was already writing that sentence in her head. I pinched the edge of the pad and felt a lift. A corner had been peeled before. The adhesive gave with a hushed sound that people mistake for quiet. Rafi brought the macro lens closer.

Under the pad, the wood read clean for two inches and then carried a pale rectangle where a sticker had lived. The outline showed sharp die-cut corners and a little downward bite at one end where someone's nail picked it up. The wood inside the rectangle carried three things. A thin film of modern adhesive. A tiny square of thermal paper no bigger than my fingernail fused to the grain. A faint print of a QR matrix, just enough dots to read as a ghost if you tilt the light. To the right, a torn string of letters stuck in the glue skin. RPL-EXLIBR.

I did not touch any of it. I set the scale and brought the lamp low. Rafi took frames from four angles and one from straight above. He shot the ghost code and the torn letters. He shot the die-cut shape. He shot the way the pad edge had been lifted before by a careless hand, not mine.

"Read me what you can," Asa said.

"Pad shows prior lift," I said. "Under it, sticker residue with die-cut corners in a modern stock. A thermal scrap fused to grain. Ghost QR pattern. Partial string reads RPL-EXLIBR. Could be a SKU for a replica ex-libris. It is the kind of label a small online seller prints for shipping or stock. Our registry base does not carry adhesive. This block does."

Gran's eyebrow climbed one notch. That is her equivalent of a curse.

I took a clean scalpel and lifted a millimeter of the thermal scrap into a sleeve. I took a micro swab of the glue film and slid it into another. The lab can tell us a binder family for adhesive and a thermal coating stock if the gods of plastic behave. Today I needed nothing more than the existence of a modern sticker ghost under a pad that should never have met a die-cut label.

Rafi flipped open his phone and showed me the photo he took last week of a replica head he found in a listing while we were building Chapter 7. The tag in the listing read Replica Ex Libris, 2 inch, museum style. The seller's code in the screenshot started with RPL. I did not say the site name. I did not need to. The rectangle under our pad said online in a way that people do not like if they love parades and plaques.

Paula leaned in, careful not to shadow the lamp. "Whoever sold this put their sticker on the base," she said. "Whoever swapped it peeled the sticker and thought they were clever."

"Clever is loud," I said. "Glue is patient."

Asa kept his voice where he keeps it when a day gives him the one small hook he wanted. "Document with the paper," he said.

I slid the Gazette closer and set the block so the sticker ghost sat above the date. Rafi shot again. He wrote the file name on the card with the time. Gran wrote the same on the ledger. We do not leave the paper out of the photo. A person who fights us later will be forced to fight a date stamp and a newsstand.

I ran my finger along the block outside the sticker ghost and felt the old grain. It did not lift. Only the rectangle carried a tack. The pad dropped back with a small sound. The edge held. I did not reseal it with any solvent. I want a lab tech to see exactly what we saw when they come with their own gloves and their own small knives.

Rafi printed a quick two-up of the live impression with the overlay and the sticker ghost with the Gazette date. He put them side by side on the board where the audit strip and the ring overlay live. People came to the counter and looked. The ones who like stories stepped closer. The ones who like numbers stayed and asked useful questions. I answered with times and shapes and the word drift.

Peppermint hopped down and sat under the board and looked up as if he approved of the aesthetic. He does not. He likes being in the center of attention and the cool tile.

I packed the head back to the vitrine, locked it while the camera watched, and let Gran write the time. Asa initialed the lock log. Paula signed as witness and went back to her bulletin map with a little smile. I love that smile. It never adds noise. It says only this: the room makes sense again.

Back at the counter, Rafi magnified the pits in the live card on the monitor and placed the H&K plate on a stand next to it. People can see difference under magnification if you ask their eyes the right question. A man from the hardware store watched for a full minute, then pointed with a rough finger.

"Your star here is missing," he said, tapping the cheek cluster with the cap on. "Three on the old. Two on the new."

"That is it," I said.

He nodded and left without asking for credit. Some people like their bit and go home.

Asa pulled his small recorder and held it toward my mouth. "Give me the one line," he said.

"Live impression under witnesses and today's paper drifts off the registry and prints a different micro pitting map," I said. "Under the base pad, we found a sticker ghost with a partial code

RPL-EXLIBR and a thermal scrap in a die-cut rectangle. That block came through someone's online shelf."

He clicked stop. He does not use adjectives when a noun will do.

Gran closed the ledger and set her palm on it for a beat. She looked at me and did not need to say careful. I had already locked the head. I had already bagged the scrap. I had already tightened the cap on the pad. She nodded.

Paula glanced at the board and then at the regulars and then at me. "What is next," she said.

"Next I call Harper and Knoll with our plate and ask for the technician's original file," I said. "Next Asa walks across to the Chamber with this two-up and asks about a tote, a driver, a pool iPad, and a sticker code."

He did not disagree. He saved his battery for the walk.

Before he left, I took one more look at the block under the lamp. The rectangle sat there in the grain with its little QR freckles and that stub of RPL-EXLIBR. It looked like the kind of stain you get when you put a hot mug on wood and pretend you will wipe it later. It will never leave. People think they can peel a label and erase a history. They cannot. Adhesive writes biographies.

I slid the two-up into a sleeve and put it at the front of the binder so we would not forget where the day had turned from talk to grip. Then I wrote the last line for the chapter card with a point that did not need flourish.

I lifted the stamp base pad.

Under it sat sticker residue from a recent online seller.

CHAPTER 16

The Spare

If a swap lives in the room, procurement lives on a screen. People forget that printers and browsers are witnesses with perfect memory when you treat them right.

We started in the office with the public workstation we keep for searches and label templates. It is not fancy. It holds a shared browser, a basic word suite, and a hard rule. No saved passwords. The Chamber breaks rules when it suits them. Celeste used this box last week to "help format" sponsor cards. I let her because I like proof more than I like peace.

Gran opened the witness ledger and wrote the time. 2:46 p.m., office workstation, browser session, printer queue. She drew a small square around workstation. She likes boxes when we hunt inside a box.

Rafi took his seat at the keyboard. Asa set his notebook on the file cabinet and watched the screen and the door at once. Peppermint jumped to the windowsill and pretended to sleep while keeping one eye on the cursor.

"Network is yours," I said to Asa.

He showed me the signed consent and the quick addendum from the DA for Chamber cloud items linked to the event. He does not wing it. He gets his paper in line before I lift a finger.

"Browser first," I said.

Rafi opened the shared profile and dug into the history cache. We lock the box down at close. The history still held last week's sessions. One bundle sat on Tuesday at 4:37 p.m. Six tabs. He restored the set and let the browser bloom. At the far left, a search page showed the query string plain.

museum replica ex-libris

Not my phrasing. The time stamp on the result page matched the router log where CR-iPad had joined Guest at 4:36, and a Chamber volunteer badge had pinged the door sensor. People travel with their habits. They type what they think.

Rafi scrolled the results. A marketplace listing sat in the top row with a thumbnail of a round die head on a wooden block. Title: Museum Replica Ex Libris, 2 inch. Seller code in the URL path began with RPL-EXLIBR. The same string we pulled from the sticker ghost under our base pad. He clicked.

The listing loaded with the speed of small sins. Wooden block with a clear pad. Die face in a generic cat crest style that would fool anyone who wants to be fooled. Options for 1.5 inch and 2 inch. Shipping in two days. A SKU field at the bottom read RPL-EXLIBR-2IN. A tiny help bubble offered a store policy for returns. The cart icon up top showed a 1 in its corner.

"Cache holds the cart," Rafi said.

"Screenshot and save," I said.

He clipped the page with the SKU and the cart count and saved the capture to our case folder with the date from the cached header. He pulled the page source. Buried in the markup, a fragment of the cart state string still held the selected option. Two inch. He dumped the source to a text file for the folder and wrote the time in the ledger.

Tab two in the restored set held a shipping calculator. Zip code typed in the field. The Chamber's hall code, not ours. Tab three held the seller's FAQ. Tab four returned to the listing. Tab five showed a checkout step with fields for email and address that had been typed and then cleared. The email field still autocompleted a hint when he clicked. ev at ch... He did not type the rest. He hit escape. I hate autofill because people trust it. Today I thanked the small demon that wrote it.

"Printer queue," I said.

Rafi opened our printer spool log for the hour Celeste sat here last week. At 4:59 p.m. the box sent a one-page print to our front laser. Title: Cart_ReplicaExLibris.pdf. User: Guest. The queue shows it exited clean. No one picked it up because we found no paper in the bin later. Someone printed it and took it. Second job, 5:02 p.m. One page. Title: Shipping_Calc.pdf. User: Guest. Exit clean. A person with neat files printed their plan. They carried it in their tote and smiled in two photos like a person who loves neat plans.

"Save the queue," I said.

Rafi exported the spool history and pinned those two lines on our wall next to the donation audit strip. One rhythm. One day. One person who tested printers like keys.

"Now the Chamber cloud," Asa said.

He had credentials for the alias group they use for events. They use a hosted suite with an admin who sets half his filters wrong and labels with colors no one can read. Asa had asked the admin to sit beside him at the Chamber office. He had his screen mirrored to ours by a simple viewer. No passwords crossed our air.

"Inbox for events at chamber," he said, eyes on his screen.

He searched for the seller domain from the marketplace and pulled up a thread with the subject Your Replica Ex Libris Has Shipped. Timestamp: two days before the event at 8:22 a.m. The message headers sat clean. From: noreply at the marketplace domain. To: events@chambercity.org. DKIM passed. SPF passed. Body simple.

Thanks for your order. Item: RPL-EXLIBR-2IN. Qty: 1. Ship to: Chamber Hall, 47 Oak. Carrier: Quickstep. Est. delivery Wed by 10 a.m. Tracking: QS-44127. Weight: 0.8 lb. Note: Base pad included.

"Open full headers," I said.

He did. Envelope shows the group address. X-Original-To shows events. List-ID shows the Chamber Events alias. Then the forward lines. The alias auto-forwarded to two members. celeste.r at chambercity.org and toby.m at chambercity.org. Both accepted at 8:23. Both read at 8:31 from the Chamber office IP.

"Save the .eml," Asa said to his admin. The man clicked Save Original and dropped the file in a folder Asa had created with the case number. He exported a PDF for my wall because he knows I love paper.

"Any order confirmation to a personal," I said.

The admin searched Celeste's mailbox within the Chamber domain. A copy of the order confirmation two days earlier sat at 8:08 a.m. The subject line matched the seller's structure. Thank you for your order. It carried the cart line. Museum Replica Ex Libris, 2 inch. It carried the same SKU. It carried a last four of a Chamber card used for payment. It carried a note. Deliver to front desk. Hold for C.R.

"Pull the receipt PDF," I said.

He did. It showed the SKU again. RPL-EXLIBR-2IN. It showed the ship to address. It showed a small thumbnail of the die with a bold placeholder Cat Crest. It showed the order ID and the exact shipping label number that matches the ghost on our wood. At the bottom, a small connection code. RPL. The same stutter we found under the base pad.

Asa kept his voice level. "Group membership," he said.

The admin opened the alias settings. Members: Celeste Rourke, owner. Toby Marris, assistant. Martin Keene, Board. Two generic roles. When the shipping notice arrived, the system forwarded to all members. He pulled the audit. Celeste clicked the tracking at 8:31 from a device flagged as CR-iPad two floors up on their office Wi-Fi. Toby opened the same link at 8:32 from a desktop in the copy room.

"Tracking page," I said.

Asa opened the carrier site with the number and pulled the path. Outbound from the seller's warehouse at 9:12 a.m. two days before. Arrival scan 8:41 a.m. on Wednesday at the Chamber Hall. Delivered 9:14 a.m. Signed by K. Avery. Janitorial. Asa toggled the sign pad image. K. Avery scrawled a K and drew a smile. He does that on everything. I have three cleaning invoices with the same flourish. We did not guess. We matched.

"Weight," Rafi said.

0.8 lb on the carrier info. Our head weighs 0.8 lb with the base block and pad. The stand alone weighs more. The conservator shipment back then weighed 4.1 lb with the case. Nothing about these numbers was slippery. They sat.

"Any outbound label the day after," I said.

The admin searched Celeste's sent mail for the seller domain. Nothing. He searched Toby's. Nothing. He searched for the carrier on return labels. One pull at 10:52 a.m. yesterday, after the fall, not before. That label went to Toby's address for a "defective product return." It was never used. The tracking shows no scan. He printed it and handed it to Asa with a face that said he did not want to be here.

"Printer queue at their office," Asa said.

The admin opened their floor queue. Two jobs printed on Wednesday at 8:55 a.m. Title: Packing slip. Title: Cat Crest Card. Both from CR-iPad. User shows Celeste. The Cat Crest Card file name aligned with the sponsor card template. The one with the ring ghost. The one from their glass. The one that sat on our counter last night with a pressure circle and a drift.

"Save the queue," I said.

He exported a CSV of the week. Asa saved it to the case folder and texted me a photo of the relevant lines because he likes me to have something on paper to hold.

We came back to our office box because I hate relying on other people's screens alone. Rafi opened the download directory on the public workstation and sorted by date. Two PDFs from Tuesday sat in the cache. Cart_ReplicaExLibris.pdf and Shipping_Calc.pdf. Same names as the jobs in our queue. Same times. Same path. He opened Cart_ReplicaExLibris.pdf. It held the listing page with the selected option and the SKU at the bottom. He opened Shipping_Calc.pdf. It held the address to the Chamber Hall and a dry run on carrier cost. He printed both to our back laser and stamped them with our date and time.

"Router entry for that hour," I said.

He pulled our router session list from Tuesday 4:30 to 5:30 and found the workstation's IP open with Peppermint Cat Guest. It is what we use when we lock the admin down. He printed the line. He printed the AMP log that tied the MAC to the box. He wrote the box label on the print. Liora Office PC. He initialed it. He writes neat when it counts.

Asa's phone buzzed. The patrol at the Chamber had found the delivery box in a recycling cart. Label still stuck to one flap like a tax. RPL-EXLIBR-2IN. He texted me a frame. The flap held a torn rectangle where a sticker had been peeled off the top of the base block. The glue ghost on our wood had the same shape. The photo and our pad could date each other like a married couple arguing about dinner.

"Chain this with the sticker ghost," I said.

Rafi printed the box flap photo and set it next to the macro of our pad residue with the QR speckle and the RPL snippet. He laid the two rulers along the edges and matched the die-cut turn. The widths sat in love. He put them in a sleeve with one caption. Box flap from Chamber recycle cart. Base pad residue from our block. Die-cut corners match.

Gran wrote her line, simple as a ruler. Search for "museum replica ex-libris" on shop workstation last week. Listing shows SKU RPL-EXLIBR-2IN. Cart printed. Ship calc printed to Chamber

Hall. Shipping email to events alias two days before. Alias forwarded to Celeste and Toby. Tracking delivered to Chamber Wednesday at 9:14 a.m. Box flap found. Sticker ghost under our pad reads RPL-EXLIBR. Chain stands.

"Anything else in the cloud," Asa said to his admin on mirror.

The man scrolled Celeste's Drive and found a folder named Event Assets. Inside, a quick note file with four bullets. Cards. Tote. Drivers. Photo. The same list I bagged from the tote pocket fifteen minutes ago. The timestamp on the Drive file sat at Tuesday 5:06 p.m. Edited from CR-iPad. He exported and printed it. He did not meet Asa's eye. He kept his face on the screen like a student who did not read and wants the quiz to end.

"Mail rule," I said.

He opened Celeste's mail rules. A rule named Quiet set to move all order confirmations to a subfolder named Receipts and mark as read. Another rule to auto forward shipping notices for events to the alias. He stared at the structure like it might save him. Asa wrote the rule names with times and initialed the page. Nothing in this stack would save anyone.

Rafi brought up the Chamber's public social in a window. Tuesday at 10:14 a.m. Celeste posted a story. A photo of a brown box on the Chamber desk with a caption New toy for history nerds. The label is out of frame. The pen next to it wears the Chamber logo. The ring of coffee on the copier glass shows in the second frame. I printed the stories with the times. She liked a crowd to feel included. Her habit gave us a step on chain we did not ask for.

Back at our box I opened our own printer queue from this morning and printed two copies of the Cart and Shipping Calc we just recovered. Anything that lives in this room lives on paper, then on drive, then in a box. I do not trust anyone's cloud not to turn to mist when heat rises.

Peppermint rose and put a paw on the keyboard like a notary seal. He pulled the laptop lid a hair and let it fall. He does that when he wants to feel useful. He is texture. I let him stamp the day.

"Assemble it," Asa said.

We laid the proof in a straight line on the counter under the camera. Browser history query for museum replica ex-libris on Tuesday at 4:37. Marketplace listing with SKU RPL-EXLIBR-2IN open. Cart and ship calc printed at 4:59 and 5:02 from our box. Chamber mail shows order confirmation at 8:08 a.m. two days before the event to the events alias. The alias forwarded to Celeste and to Toby at 8:23. Tracking delivered to the Chamber at 9:14 a.m. Wednesday. Box flap in recycle cart with the die-cut label. Pad under our block carries the sticker ghost with RPL-EXLIBR. The live impression drifts and the micro pits disagree. The driver in the tote fits the shelf lip. The tote pins lost a star at our back door. The CR-iPad woke our Guest at 5:58 and at 7:05. The hand that searched here brought the spare there and stood in our alley while our router remembered it.

Gran wrote the end line in the ledger and put a dot next to it like a period with weight. Procurement found. Two days before. Delivered to Chamber. Handled by Celeste. Mirrored to Toby.

I called the Chamber admin and asked one clean question while Asa listened.

"Who owns the events alias," I said.

"Celeste," he said. "She added Toby last fall. She kept Martin because he wants to watch."

"Who reads the mail first," I said.

"Celeste," he said. "Every time."

"Who printed on CR-iPad," I said.

"Celeste," he said.

He did not like where his own words put him. He signed Asa's export anyway and handed over the .eml. That is the part that matters.

Peppermint settled again. Rafi taped the new pieces to the wall in order. Asa took a copy of the two-page assemble with him and looked toward Oak. He had a meeting on a sidewalk with a man who calls himself a steward. He likes to hold paper like a cold pack against a lie.

At the door, he turned back. He wanted the one sentence for his record, the one he will read to a judge clean.

"Give it to me," he said.

"Celeste used our public box last week to search for 'museum replica ex-libris,' added a 2 inch to cart, printed the cart and shipping calc, then ordered it to the Chamber Hall through the events alias two days before the event," I said. "The shipping notice hit that alias and auto-forwarded to Celeste and to her assistant, Toby Marris."

He left with that line and did not look back.

CHAPTER 17

Timeline Lock

The circle table is where rumor dies. Paper owns the room. Time takes the chair at the head. I set the binder down and laid out each piece like clean plates before a meal you do not intend to enjoy.

Gran stood by the clock with the witness ledger open. Asa took the chair that lets him watch the door and the board without turning his head. Rafi ran the projector and kept his mouth shut. Paula held a pencil and did not write. Peppermint coiled on the moderator's chair with one eye on the table and one on the shaft of sun that walked across the floor.

"Read the frame," Asa said.

"Router. Tool. Tote," I said. "Plus the stamp and the glass."

I taped the first strip at the top of the whiteboard. Router log, Tuesday and event night.

"Tuesday 4:37 p.m.," I said. "Public workstation here in our office opens a browser, searches museum replica ex-libris, restores tabs, prints cart and ship calc. At 5:58 p.m. day of event, CR-iPad associates to Peppermint Cat Guest. At 7:05 p.m., same device pings again. Not a full handshake. A cached reach. Enough to prove a body stood in our back pocket while we worked the chaos window."

Rafi put the two router screenshots side by side. The lines glowed in that washed blue I trust more than a throat. Gran copied times into the ledger with the steady hand that taught a town to read.

"Tool," I said, and held up the macro of the press base.

We ran the bench photos in sequence on the screen. Three old screws, one new. Fresh bite on threads at the front right. Washer burnish ring bright. Slot burr glittering like a cheap ring. Shelf lip above the press with a driver scrape and a twin striation gap. Then the clear-handled flat driver from the Chamber tote on our staff hook. Shank scuff lines at the same spacing. Tip smear that fits the slot wall on the new head.

"New screw at front right lets the base pivot around the left front foot," I said. "Wax on that foot proves the pivot point. The swing writes the same arc as the dust swipe on the shelf. The fall lives where the arc leads."

"Say the why," Asa said.

"Because someone wanted a topple that looked like age," I said. "Tap, not throw. Loosen one corner. Leave the rest to play old. Build a stage and push a shelf when no one watches."

"Tote," I said, and touched the sleeve with the enamel star.

We pinned the alley still from the title office and the star pin we lifted under our back rack. The still shows the Chamber tote at 6:58. Gap in the pin cluster where the star should be. Our frame of the Chamber's morning post shows the star present on Celeste's tote at ten fourteen. The afternoon balloons photo shows it present at 4:12. Our still at 6:58 shows the gap. Our floor holds the fallen star, bent post and torn clutch three inches apart. Chips at the point. The tote hung low while a body waited by our back door at 6:58 through 7:07. Router remembers that body at 7:05.

"Window," I said, and turned the task lamp toward the bay photos on the lower rail.

The crack origin sits inside the pane. The interior track carries a fresh crescent scrape at thirty two inches that matches the spring gate on a Chamber lanyard clasp. The rug at the rack holds red nylon filaments that twin the spare lanyard bundle they left. The sill carries a red filament too. The ring on our counter glass is small with a nick at twenty degrees. The sponsor cards in our stack carry a bigger ring with a nick at thirty five that matches the Chamber copier glass ring they have ignored for a year. Their own feed shows the ring on their glass in a selfie where Celeste felt cute about a box. The donor cards we pulled from our pile carry that same ghost.

"Stamp," I said, and kept my voice flat as a ruler.

Registry card from ten years back shows a micro flat at the ear tip and a small diagnostic nick at the ring near ten. Conservator's photo shows the same. Our blind bite in Chapter 7 shows a drift. Our live impression today shows the same drift with ink. Ear prints sharp, not flat. Micro pitting map disagrees in three zones. Under the base pad we lifted a sticker ghost with a fragment RPL-EXLIBR and a faint QR speckle. Chamber recycle cart holds the delivery box flap with a die-cut rectangle where that sticker lived. Their events alias received the shipping confirmation two days before. It auto forwarded to Celeste and to her assistant, Toby Marris. Their cart printed. Their ship calc printed. The carrier delivered Wednesday at 9:14 a.m. Signed by the janitor who draws a smiley in his name. They printed on CR-iPad at 8:55 that morning. Packing slip. Cat Crest Card.

I set each sleeve in order on the table. Router at the top, tool and tote and window in the middle, stamp at the bottom like a foundation. Gran wrote the bones in the ledger while Paula watched the overlay sit on the fresh impression and drift by a hair from ten to two like a compass that forgot home.

"Now read the minutes," Asa said.

I pulled the paper strip I keep for this job. It is a five minute ladder from 6:10 to 6:25. We wrote the markers longhand. This town can handle a line that reads clean.

"6:11," I said. "RBK LAST on the espresso till. 6:12, VOID SLIP 0174. 6:12, donation printer reprints 174 as a top copy. Shoulder with leather strap reaches to keys. Strap flash fits Celeste. No staff at island."

"6:15," I said. "Guestbook moved for flow by Celeste. Barium dust line across spine. Key ring in cup spins a quarter. My dust bows to her hand and tells on it."

"6:19," I said. "Back chime sounds. Nina on mic under tent. Bria at Square. Harold on his tape. Paula at the cones. No one we cleared can swing iron. The figure at the bay frame hears the spoon ping the jar inside the tent. We all do. Noise moves. Nerves wait."

"6:21," I said. "Thud in the hall. Ladder lies at the travel shelf. Press leaps. One foot wears citrus wax from the front lane. The opposite foot clean. The base pivots where a new screw frees it. A body falls. We call time."

"6:40," I said. "Front camera shows a silhouette at the pane with the tote strap long. The cluster gap is visible. Martin says he saw Celeste leave at 6:05. The camera decides his memory is a blanket he used to sleep."

"6:58," I said. "Title office camera sees a figure with a Chamber tote enter our alley slice. No face. Cluster gap sits where a star should be. The figure waits under our awning near the back door, next to the rack where we found the star."

"7:05," I said. "Router notes the CR-iPad associate blink. Not a full handshake. A cached reach."

"7:07," I said. "Figure leaves. Star lies on our concrete with the bent post and the torn clutch."

I let the board breathe for a long ten count. People who try to talk early learn the room does not admire elbows.

"Assemble your line," Asa said.

"Celeste procured a two inch replica head through the Chamber events alias two days before, brought it to the hall on Wednesday morning, and printed her packing slip and card templates on CR-iPad," I said. "Yesterday she carried her tote and her lanyard into our shop, stood at our counter and our bay, moved our guestbook and touched our key, staged an inside crack on the pane with a clasp scrape on the track, printed a top copy of a donation slip at 6:12 without tender, and stood near the hall at 6:19 when the back chime rang. The press had been loosened at the front right with a small driver from the Chamber tote on our hook. At 6:21, the press toppled and the ladder swung. At 6:58, a figure with her tote stood by our back door. At 7:05, CR-iPad remembered us. At 7:07, the figure left. Later this morning, the live impression under witnesses drifted off the registry and printed the wrong pits. Under the base pad we found the sticker ghost from a seller that calls the SKU RPL-EXLIBR. Their box flap in the Chamber cart carries the same die-cut footprint. Their copier glass prints a coffee ring ghost on their cards. Our sponsor cards wear that ring. Our counter ring does not match. The tote lost a star under our rack, and their social shows that star pinned before the event."

Rafi lined the one-page summary he printed with each sentence on one line. He laid a pencil on it so Asa could draw his own dots. Asa did not draw. He reads and remembers. Then he looked at me and asked the only fair question left.

"Why the blackout," he said.

"To build the shove and the swing without faces," I said. "To let a trip and a topple read as an accident. To give a new screw the same voice as an old house. Also to control a vote. Also to shift attention, because shifting attention is a hobby she practices."

He did not argue. He does not water a field when the crop is already cut.

Paula spoke for the first time. "Could a shove be panic," she said.

"Panic follows a plan when a plan hits a wall," I said. "She planned a swap and a reveal. She planned a reprint. She planned a pane move to the Chamber hall. She planned a driver in a tote.

The shove fit the plan. The fall did not."

Gran wrote Panic follows a plan on the ledger and underlined plan, not panic.

Asa closed his notebook. He looked at each plate on the table like a person moving a level across a shelf to see if the bubble sits where it should. His face did not change. He does not reward the neatness of other people's work. He uses it.

"Call him in," he said.

Rafi had texted Toby earlier to come by as a volunteer who wants to help tidy the tent. Toby arrived with a cautious step and both hands visible. He is young in that way that makes people give him free advice even when he did not ask. He glanced at the board and then at the chair backs and then at Asa. He sat where Asa pointed, across from the tote star and the live stamp impression.

"Toby," Asa said. "You see what is on this table."

"I see printouts," he said.

"You see a plan," I said.

He looked at me. He knows me. I have loaned him a tape gun twice. He looked at the star sleeve. His eye did a small skip. He blinked and forced his gaze to the top strip instead. The router lines do not scare him. The metal scares him. The star scares him because it points without raising its voice.

"We are giving you one chance to tell the sequence without trying to keep your supervisor's dignity intact," Asa said.

Toby's mouth moved without sound. People think honesty is a choice you make all at once. It is not. It happens in small lurches that feel like tripping. He reached for a sentence and found a flat field.

"Celeste ran the plan alone," he said. "She ordered. She printed. She told me to carry boxes. She asked me to loosen a screw on the press after she saw the dust on the shelf. I did not. I told her I could not. She laughed and said you are sweet. Then she took a phone call. That is all I know."

The sentence sat in the air like a plank laid across a ditch. It held for one foot. It would not hold for two. His eye flicked again to the sleeve with the star. A small, fast glance. The kind of glance a child gives a cookie he claims he did not touch.

"Look at the ring," I said, and pointed to the sponsor card ghost from the Chamber copier. He looked. He did not know what to do with a ring. He tried to smile. I saved him from himself.

"Look at the star," I said, and pointed to the sleeve. He did. His face said what his mouth did not. He had reached into a tote and felt a chip.

Asa kept his tone mild. "Who packed the tote after the meeting last month," he said.

"Everyone," Toby said, too fast.

"Names," Asa said.

"Celeste," he said, slower. "Me. Martin. The intern with the green jacket. The janitor took the boxes after."

"Who set the drivers on the table," Asa said.

"Celeste," he said.

"Who keeps the CR-iPad charged," Asa said.

"I do," he said. "She uses it."

"Who printed on it Wednesday," Asa said.

"She did," he said.

"Who asked you for a return label yesterday," Asa said.

"She did," he said. "I printed it. We did not use it."

"Why," Asa said.

"She fell," he said. The word came out small and blunt.

Rafi put the printed order confirmation next to the shipping notice. He placed the box flap photo above the sticker ghost under our pad. He did not say a word. He does not need to. People read easier when the table says the sentence for them.

"Tell me where you were at 6:19," I said.

"In the copy room," he said. "We had a paper jam. I called the vendor line and left a message. You can check the phone log."

"Tell me where you were at 7:05," I said.

"Walking past the back door with trash," he said. "I saw a shape. I did not speak."

"You did not speak," I said. "But your device did." I tapped the router line.

He looked at the strip and could not help himself. He looked at the star again. The glance was shorter. The fear in it had more weight.

"Celeste ran the plan alone," he said again, softer.

"Plans do not swing iron," I said. "Hands do."

He shut his mouth. Asa let the quiet live. He is good at that. Gran clicked her pen once and stopped. Paula did not move. Peppermint watched a dust mote and flicked one ear.

"If you turned a screw," Asa said to Toby, "you will say that now."

Toby shook his head. He held it too long for the denial to mean no. He has not learned how to make his body support a lie. He will. I hope he does not.

"Then you held the ladder while someone else did," I said. "Or you held the tote. Or you held the door. Or you held your breath and pretended a driver scraping a shelf lip was not the sound you heard."

His shoulders twitched. You can mistake that for a flinch if you like. I did not. I called it a memory trying to push through pride.

"Asa will pull your phone's location history and the Chamber's hallway camera," I said. "If you want your part to read as late regret instead of early greed, you will set it in ink now."

He looked at the live stamp impression on the card we pressed at 2:13. He looked at the overlay. He looked at the registry photo. He looked at the sticker ghost. His eyes tried to climb the board to the router line where no feelings live. He failed. He looked back at the star. His right hand made a small grabbing motion at his thigh, the way a hand remembers grabbing something that had points.

"Celeste ran the plan," he said, and swallowed. "I helped carry the tote. I did not touch the press."

"Who did," Asa said.

He stared at the table. He has a gentle mouth. It would fare poorly in a courtroom. He will have a better day if he learns how to keep it closed. Today, the mouth opened.

"She said the wall scuff looked bad," he said. "She said a toppled press would explain it and make a story. She said optics again. She used that word. She took the small driver and reached up. I told her not to. I told her not to. I did not touch it. I did not. I held the tote because it kept sliding. The pins scraped the shelf."

"Which pins," I said.

"The star," he said without wanting to. His eyes flicked to the sleeve and stayed there like a magnet found its home.

"You saw it fall," I said.

"I felt it catch," he said. "Then later I found the clutch in the dust and threw it away. I did not see the star fall. I did not look. I am not a monster."

"You stood at the back door at 6:58," Asa said.

"I took trash," he said. He could not stop himself from answering. "She was there."

"At 7:05 your device remembered our Guest," Asa said.

"I walked by," he said. "I did not connect."

"CR-iPad connected twice," Asa said. "At 5:58 and at 7:05 it reached."

He pressed his lips together. He did not argue. He looked to the router again as if the strip might have mercy. The strip does not.

"Did you know about the replica," I said.

"I saw the box," he said. "I signed nothing. I saw the pad. She peeled a sticker off and stuck it to the flap. I carried the box to the back room. She told me to recycle later."

Rafi slid the box flap photo closer. He did not smile. He rarely does.

"Who printed the reprint at 6:12," I said.

"I saw her reach in," he said. "I did not tell her to stop. I did not know what the keys did. I know now."

"Who moved the guestbook at 6:15," I said.

"She did," he said. "She said flow. She said it three times. It is how she talks when she is excited."

I let that sit while the room exhaled its agreement. The ledger had the word flow written twice on one page. The word had earned no friends.

Asa leaned back one inch. He does that when he decides a line has held enough weight to carry into the hallway. He stood and gathered three sheets only. Live impression with drift. Driver macro with shelf lip scrape. Alley still with tote gap and the star sleeve taped to the bottom edge.

"You will write a statement," he said to Toby. "You will say what you touched and what you saw. You will bring your phone. You will not speak to anyone at the Chamber before you speak to me again."

Toby nodded like a person who wants to be told what to do. He will do it. People who are not monsters often do.

He stood and then sat again without meaning to. His eyes went once more to the star. The flick was small and quick and honest. The body remembers when a point bites.

He left with Asa and the room felt the kind of quiet I like. Gran closed the ledger and set her palm on the cover for a breath. Rafi pulled the projector cable and took the router lines down. The wall stayed heavy with the rest. Paula set her pencil on the table and looked at me with a face that said the town can handle this if we keep it simple.

"Read the sentence," she said.

"Router to CR-iPad, press to the new screw, window crack to inside, ghost ring to the Chamber copier," I said. "Tote to the star."

She nodded. She likes tidy. So do I.

Peppermint slid off the moderator's chair and walked a slow lap around the table like a judge who likes to think with his paws. He paused by the star sleeve and blinked at the chip. He does not solve. He annotates.

I pulled the chapter card and wrote the last line for the file with the words that will hold in court and in a kitchen and in a hall full of people who have opinions.

The board merged tech, tool, and tote. Asa called Toby in. Toby said Celeste ran the plan alone. When his eyes touched the star, they told the truth.

CHAPTER 18

Assistant Cracks

Back office, two chairs, one table. No window. No applause. Just air that smells like paper and citrus, and a recorder with a red light that cares nothing for nerves.

Gran opened the witness ledger at the counter and wrote the time. 3:18 p.m., back office, statement from Toby Marris. She slid the ledger to the edge so I could see it if I needed the date to steady my hand. Rafi stood by the door with a legal pad and the kind of patience that makes a room honest. Asa sat across from Toby and kept his shoulders quiet. His quiet is a tool.

Peppermint settled on the file cart outside the open door where he could be near and not in the way. Texture, not help.

I set four sleeves on the table within Toby's sightline, not in a pile, in a row. The star pin in its bag. The macro of the shelf lip scrape with the twin lines. The clear-handled flat driver from the Chamber tote. The live impression card we pressed an hour ago with today's paper in the frame, its ring drifting off the registry overlay by a hair.

"Recorder on," Asa said.

The click lived in the room a second, then sat down.

I did not start with questions. Questions give people room to rehearse. I gave him a sentence and let him decide if he wanted to be part of this town or part of someone else's story.

"You skim donors by swapping the stamp and rolling receipts," I said. "You stage a crack in our window to justify moving the exhibit to the Chamber hall so you can control the chain. You loosen the press to hide the scuff you left on our shelf when you swapped. The chime cut spooked you. The press fell when Celeste grabbed the shelf."

His mouth went dry. I watched him want to argue with one word and then another, pick none, and swallow instead. He is not built for lies that require choreography.

"Tell me where I am wrong," I said.

He glanced at Asa. Asa did not blink. He looked at the driver in the sleeve. His eye hung on the tip, the little smear on one wing where metal met slot and skidded. His fingers twitched once on his thigh where people keep tools in a pocket they should not fill.

"I did not plan it," he said. "I am not that person."

"That will matter later," I said. "Right now the room needs a map."

He exhaled and tapped his own knee once like he wished it were the table. He stared at the pin bag as if a point could forgive him.

"Tuesday," I said, and slid the print of our workstation browser history across the table. The query line sat at the top. museum replica ex-libris. "She used our box. She printed the cart. She printed the ship calculator. The Chamber events alias got the order and sent the shipping notice two days before. The alias forwarded to Celeste and to you. We have the .eml. We have the tracking. We have the box flap from your recycling cart with the die-cut footprint. We have the sticker ghost under the pad with RPL-EXLIBR in the glue skin."

He nodded once, a small nod that looked like gravity, not agreement.

"She said it was a prop," he said. "She said donors love props. She said the real stamp was too precious to handle in public. She said moving the exhibit to the Chamber would protect it and make our hall feel like a museum. She said it too many times."

"Did you read the order on your phone," Asa said.

"Yes," he said. "She forwarded the shipping to my inbox from the alias. I clicked the tracking in the hallway. My mail app still has the alias logged in. You can look."

"Phone, please," Asa said.

Toby placed his phone on the table like he was surrendering a pocketknife at a courthouse. He unlocked without being told and pushed the mail icon. Asa leaned in just enough to see the accounts list. events@chambercity.org sat under his personal address, toggled on. Last activity, Wednesday 8:31 a.m. He opened the shipping notice. The header showed the alias. The forward line showed Celeste. The link inside showed the Quickstep tracking we had already pulled on Asa's screen from the Chamber office. He did not fight it. He placed the phone back down and folded his hands.

"Wednesday morning," I said. "Box arrives at the Chamber desk. You carry it. Then what."

"We opened it in the copy room," he said. "She peeled the sticker off the base and stuck it on the flap. She said people would notice and that would ruin the photo. She laughed. I hated that laugh."

"You did not throw the sticker away," I said.

"I threw the flap in the cart," he said. "The sticker stayed on the flap. I did not think about it again."

"You thought about the tote," I said.

He rubbed two fingers together, skin against skin, like he was trying to rub off glue that had dried last week.

"She said load the tote," he said. "Cards, drivers, pins, lanyards. She wanted the bowl of clear screwdrivers on the table next to the candy dish. She said people love free tools. She called them charming."

He looked at the driver sleeve. He did not touch it. He has learned not to touch inside a ring of paper.

"Yesterday," I said. "Start at five."

"We set the tables," he said. "She walked with me and Tessa and Martin. She did not talk to the janitor. He signed for something else and left. At five fifty-five she told me to stand straight and smile and keep the tote near. At six she told me to carry the tote through the room. She said movement makes a space feel full."

"At 6:11," I said, and tapped the till strip on our board, "she reached over our island, hit RBK and VOID, and reprinted a donation slip. You were where."

"Copy room," he said. "I had a jam. I called the vendor line and cursed under my breath and hung up. You can pull the call log."

"At 6:12 the donation printer spit a top copy," I said. "Then she moved the guestbook at 6:15 and brushed our key. She used the word flow."

He closed his eyes a second like the word hurt. "She says flow when she thinks she is clever," he said.

"Now the crack," I said.

He opened his eyes. He could not pretend he did not know which crack.

"She bumped the sill with her tote and then pulled the lanyard clasp along the track," he said. "She said there, optics, see, the pane is unsafe here."

"She made the scrape," I said.

"Yes," he said. "She did. And then she turned it into an argument for moving the case to the Chamber. She called it a safety issue. She told Martin to make a show of concern."

"She told you to loosen the press after that," I said.

He looked at the driver again. He tried a small lie and it died before it reached his mouth.

"Yes," he said. "She said the dust arc above the press looked like a grab. She said if the press tipped later it would hide that. She said it would be written off as age. She said we would roll the exhibit out, close the books, and no one would know the difference. She said this is how events work when you want engagement. She used the word engage."

He swallowed and touched his own throat like his voice had snagged on a nail.

"She said loosen a foot so the base would give with a hand," he said. "She handed me a clear-handled driver from the tote."

"Which foot," Asa said.

"Front right," he said. "I could not move the others. That one turned. I felt it give. A quarter turn, maybe a half, I do not know. The washer sang a little. The slot scraped. I missed once and the shaft hit the shelf. That is your mark."

I slid the macro of the shelf lip closer. He flinched. His eyes measured the twin lines and then found the driver sleeve without wanting to. He looked away like a child trying not to stare at a cut.

"Her tote pins scraped the lip while you worked," I said.

"Yes," he said. "The star caught once. I felt it. I did not watch it fall. I kept the tote against my hip and pressed the driver and did not breathe."

He ran his fingers along the seam of the chair like the metal needed calming.

"At 6:19 the chime rang," I said. "Where were you."

"In the copy room doorway," he said. "She was in the hall. She told me to hold steady and not look stupid. She said go stand at the bay and ask Paula where to put the cards while she got the key."

My stomach did a small swing. I do not like how much she enjoyed her little words for people. I kept my face flat.

"At 6:21 the press fell," I said.

"I heard it," he said. "I did not see the exact moment. I saw the ladder move and then the press slam and then I saw Celeste on the floor and then I tasted metal in my mouth."

"Lights," Asa said.

"On," he said. "We had not cut them yet. She wanted the cut at seven for the move. She said we would make a show of lifting the case and walking it across the room while Nina said a line about town pride. She said it twice on Tuesday while I made the list."

He looked at the live impression card as if it would offer him a softer story. It did not. It drifted off the overlay and told the truth in a small, stubborn way.

"After the fall," I said, "you printed a return label."

"Yes," he said. "She told me to do it while people cried and while you ran the back. She said defective product, quick, quick, quick. I opened the alias on my phone and printed from the desktop in the copy room. Then I froze. I could not walk to the box. I could not do any more."

He stared at the table. His right hand rose an inch, shaped like it wanted a pen, and then fell back to his thigh.

"What was the plan with receipts," I said.

He did not look up. He picked at the skin near his thumb where a person chews when they feel like they should apologize to the air.

"She kept the top copies she reprinted on your island," he said. "She said she would clean the donation log by running a rollback and a void and then reprint top copies as if a donor needed a clean sheet. She said a sponsor never notices the difference between a first strike and a reprint if the number matches the slip. She said we would fill envelopes after and nobody would go looking for the original because the binder would show completeness and that satisfies people."

He lifted his eyes. He looked like a person who wants to sleep for a week.

"Then the press fell," he said, softer. "After that there was no we. There was only noise."

"Did you touch the stamp head," I said.

He shook his head. "I carried a box of cards," he said. "She touched the head. She pressed it at the Chamber on Wednesday morning to test the bite. On her desk. Not in the hall. Not under lights. She wanted to make sure. She smiled when it printed dark. She said it would sell the story."

"Your phone shows the alias login," Asa said. "Your driver wing smear meets the slot. Your shank gap meets the shelf twin lines. Your hand held the tote with the star that fell under our back rack. At 7:05 your device walked past our door and the CR-iPad blinked from under someone's arm. Are you still alone in this."

He stared at his wrists like they had written his name on something he could not erase.

"She ran it," he said. "I followed. I turned a screw."

"Thank you," Asa said.

It was not praise. It was a receipt. He took his notebook and wrote three lines in a row and did not look at Toby while he wrote. He lets people keep their faces while their words go on paper. It is kinder than it sounds.

I turned to the live impression again because I like ending a paragraph with a fact. I placed the registry photo beside it and set the overlay pins in the holes. The flat on the ear on the registry sat where the flat should sit. Our ear printed sharp. The ring drifted by a hair. The pits in the cheek argued with history. I took a fresh photo because I keep proof near the surface when a room breathes lies out and truth in.

"Say the sequence in your words," I said to Toby. "No edits. No sales pitch. Timeline and verbs."

He took a breath, looked at the recorder light, and kept his voice in a narrow lane.

"Tuesday Celeste used your computer to search for a replica stamp and printed the cart and shipping calculator," he said. "She placed the order to the Chamber through the events alias. Wednesday the box arrived. We opened it. She peeled the sticker. I carried the box to the copy room. She pressed a test in her office. Thursday we set up. At 6:11 she reprinted a donation slip at your island using rollback and void. At 6:15 she moved your guestbook and brushed your key. She scraped the window track to make an excuse to move the case. She told me to loosen the front right screw on the press to hide the dust mark. I loosened it. I scraped your shelf lip with the shaft. The tote pins caught the lip. The star pin probably fell later when we stood at the back. At 6:19 the chime rang. At 6:21 the press fell when she grabbed the shelf. After that I printed a return label and did nothing else."

He stopped and put his hands flat on his knees. He did not cry. He did not wobble. He sat like a person who had finally said the sentence he should have said at noon and hated every word.

Asa looked at the driver sleeve and the macro and Toby's phone. He does a simple thing at the end of a good hour. He puts his pencil down and lets the air find its level.

"I will need your written statement," he said. "You will sign it. You will bring your phone to the station so we can image it. You will not delete a thing. You will not call anyone at the Chamber. You will sit tight and wait for your attorney before you talk to anyone besides me."

Toby stared at the recorder and then at Asa and then at the door where Gran's ledger sat behind the counter like a person. He swallowed and pushed one terrible word into the room.

"Deal," he said. "Can I get a deal."

Asa's face did not flex.

"That is later," he said. "Not here."

Toby nodded. He looked at the star one last time. His eye did the small flick I clocked in the circle. It is what guilt does when it finds a single point it cannot ignore.

I stood and closed the sleeve on the driver and the macro and the live card. I slid the star back in the evidence box. I let the box close with a soft sound. No thud. No theater. Only paper and a clasp.

Rafi opened the door and Peppermint jumped down from the cart and padded past Toby's shoe without interest. The cat paused, sniffed the chair leg where Toby's hand had rested, and kept walking as if the smell held nothing he needed. He is honest. He likes warm spots.

Gran wrote the last line in the ledger in that small, square way that keeps a town from drifting. Toby Marris admits loosening front right screw to hide shelf scuff, confirms alias access on phone, confirms sequence of reprint and window scrape. Requests deal. Asa declines for now.

The recorder clicked off. The room got larger. The story got smaller. Good.

CHAPTER 19

Charges Split

Night pulled even with the storefront and held. The squad cars idled at the curb with their light bars turned down to a slow pulse. Red, then blue, then calm. The cones at the bay stayed where Paula left them. Our board still covered the counter with times and faces and lines you could follow with a finger. The door stood open for air. The sidewalk took the weight.

Asa chose the sidewalk for the readout because ink lands better in public than in a back room. People hear the same words at the same time. No rumor gets a head start.

Gran locked the till and brought the witness ledger anyway. She set it on the book truck by the door like a table at a polling place. Rafi stacked sleeves in the case box in the order we would hand them to evidence. Paula parked a chair by the threshold for anyone who felt weak. She never uses the word faint. She says sit if you need it. People sit.

Peppermint moved up into the bay, nose pressed to the pane, eyes on the street. He blinked twice at the slow lights and stayed still. Texture, not help.

The circle formed without theater. Vendors from the tent. The neighbor who heard the chime. Nina with her jaw set. Harold with a white paper bag he handed to Rafi without comment.

Bria with her pouch zipped shut for once. Martin, buttoned and pale. Two Chamber board members who had called each other three times already. The janitor, K Avery, with his hands in his back pockets and a line of dried cleaner's powder on one cuff. He draws a smile in his K. Even tonight that signature lived. Town.

Asa stepped to the curb edge where the light touched his shoulder and not his face. He read from a clipboard, not because he needed it, because the paper makes people listen. He kept the sentences short. People remember short.

"Charges," he said. "Toby Marris, tampering with evidence and obstruction."

Toby stood between two uniforms by the hydrant. No cuffs. Not yet. He had given a statement. He had handed over his phone without fight. His eyes stayed on the board on our counter like a student who did not plan to pass and now hopes for extra credit.

Asa lifted one page from the packet and held it up where the squad camera saw it.

"Tampering," he said. "Front right screw of the press loosened to alter the condition of a scene. Obstruction, reprint label for return of a replica stamp head after a fatal fall and concealment actions related to donation paperwork. Both supported by physical marks, device logs, and a sworn statement."

He set the page under his arm and glanced once at me. I kept my face flat. No victory. Nothing here felt like a win.

"Death ruling," he said. "Celeste Rourke, negligent homicide attached to a staged cover, ruled by the medical examiner based on injury pattern, swing path physics, and witness accounts. A toppled press loosened to mask a shelf scuff, a ladder swing during a staged blackout rehearsed for a show move, a fall that followed. The plan created the hazard. The hazard killed."

He did not say her name loud. He did not have to. The board members looked at each other and then at the ground. One of them lifted a sleeve cuff and pressed his knuckle to his upper lip like a man checking a tooth. People want to fix what hurts with small motions. Nothing on that curb wanted to be fixed.

"Civic complaint," Asa said. "Filed with the city manager and the cultural affairs officer at four forty this afternoon. It names the Chamber for mishandling public artifacts, failure to maintain custody chain, and unsafe practices during an event. The complaint triggers a review of their event protocols, their access controls, and any use of pool devices to manipulate systems off-site."

The board members started to speak. He lifted a palm. Not the stop of a traffic cop. A cleaner sign that said hold it. He finished his sentence.

"Tonight we keep this simple," he said. "Evidence transfers and statements only. The rest has its own room and its own clock."

He nodded at me. My turn.

I stepped forward with the case box and laid three items on the truck, not for show, for chain. The macro of the front right screw and the shelf scrape. The live impression card with the overlay drift and the Gazette date. The alley still with the tote gap and the star bag taped under it.

I spoke one line for each, the way a clerk learns to at a board meeting when people have twenty items and no patience.

"Tool," I said. "New screw at front right. Fresh bite in threads. Shelf lip scrape with twin lines. Small driver from the Chamber tote carries the same shank gap. Tip smear matches the slot. Base pivot fits the wax transfer on the opposite foot and the swing path."

"Stamp," I said. "Live impression under witnesses drifts off the registry by a hair and prints the wrong pit map. Under the base pad, sticker ghost with RPL-EXLIBR and a QR speckle. Recycle cart across the street holds the box flap with the matching die-cut shape. Chamber cloud shows the order to the events alias two days before. The alias forwarded to Celeste and to Toby."

"Tote," I said. "Title office camera caught a figure with the Chamber tote at 6:58 to 7:07. Cluster gap where a star pin was.

We recovered the star under the back rack. Chamber socials show the star in place on Celeste's tote earlier. Router shows CR-iPad at 5:58 and again at 7:05. Device remembered our Guest from the alley."

I kept my voice even and my hands close to the board. No flourish. The curb did not need it.

Asa lifted his clipboard once more. "The pad found under the stamp base carried glue from a die-cut sticker," he said, for people who needed the words from a badge. "The sticker code fragment matches the seller code on the order confirmation. That confirmation came to the events alias. The shipping notice hit the same alias. The alias forwards to two people. We have logs for both reads."

Celeste's cousin, a soft-voiced woman from the board whose name I do not use in this room, put a hand on her mouth. She did not cry. She whispered nothing. She stood with her hand on her mouth and stared at the curb seam like it might tell a kinder version. It will not.

Rafi passed two evidence sleeves to the patrol tech and read off the numbers from the tags so the camera could take the echo. He slid the driver into a transport box with foam and did not look at Toby while he did it. He will not give the room a small theater if the room can live without it.

Nina stepped one pace closer to the truck. "I want it on the record that I stayed on a taped X at the mic," she said, voice clean.

"It is on the record," Asa said. "Tent feed and Square logs lock it in."

She nodded once, nothing smug in it, then took a half step back so the neighbor could move forward.

K Avery pointed at the star bag, then at his own shirt cuff. "I signed for the box Wednesday," he said. "I took it to the desk and walked away. I did not open it. I did not open anything. I have enough work to do without pushing paper I do not get paid for."

"No one said you did," Asa said.

"People say," he said.

"I do not," Asa said.

K Avery gave a short shrug and went back to the cluster of volunteers near the lamp post. He does not need town theater. He wanted one clean line he could carry home.

Martin opened his mouth and then closed it. He took off his glasses and cleaned the lenses with the tail of his shirt, then put them back on and kept his eyes on his shoes. He told us earlier that Celeste left at 6:05. He has not repeated it since the camera told him he bluffed himself. He will need to live with the new time for a while. That is his work, not mine.

Harold passed the paper bag to me. I gave it to Rafi. Inside, four pastries. I lifted one and handed it to Nina without comment. She took it and split it into two for the neighbor and the janitor. Town does that even when the night tastes like copper.

Paula checked the faces and moved the chair an inch forward so an older woman who had done eighty minutes on her feet could sit without feeling watched. Paula is the kind of person who puts chairs in the right place for other people's bones. It carries a room without anyone noticing.

Asa turned to Toby. "State your name for the record," he said.

"Toby Marris," he said.

"State your employment," Asa said.

"Chamber assistant," he said.

"State your charges," Asa said.

"Tamp... tampering with evidence and obstruction," he said, throat rough.

"You have counsel," Asa said.

"He is on his way," Toby said.

"You will be processed at the station and released on conditions if your counsel secures it," Asa said. "You will not access any Chamber systems. You will not move property related to events. You will not contact members named in this complaint without going through counsel."

Toby nodded. His eyes kept moving to the star bag. He does not want to. He cannot stop. The body keeps its own timeline.

Asa raised the clipboard to chest height again and faced the board members. "The complaint does not handcuff your operations," he said. "It forces a hold on artifact handling while the review runs. Lock the pool iPads in your safe. Seal the tote supply and the drivers. Inventory the lanyards. Pull your copier for service and clean the glass. Adopt sign-out procedures for display keys. Put your event rules on paper with signatures. That is the corrective path. You will follow it."

One of the board members started to say that the Chamber has standards. Asa cut him off with a look. Not a glare. A quiet no. The man stopped. He will say it later on a platform with a logo behind him. Tonight his mouth stayed shut.

Gran turned one page in the ledger and wrote a short line in the square hand she reserves for moments that will need to live longer than we will. Charges split. Negligent homicide ruling. Civic complaint filed. Board instructed on corrective path. She signed her initials and set her pen down with that little click that tells my heart we are still running a shop, not a stage.

The patrol tech finished the photo round on the sidewalk. He shot the board in the window for the case file. He shot the truck with the sleeves. He shot my hand holding the live impression in frame with the Gazette date. He shot the driver bag on the foam. He read off the tag numbers again for the recorder. Then he nodded at Asa. Transfer done.

The medical examiner's courier, a woman I see twice a year and always wish I did not, stepped forward without stepping into the cone of the squad lights. She spoke soft and precise.

"Cause of death, blunt force head trauma consistent with fall against industrial hardware," she said. "Contributing factor, loss of balance during sudden movement in a tight aisle. Scene reconstruction provided by your team supports a swing initiated by a toppled press. Ruling, negligent homicide attached to a staged condition. I will have the file to you at 09:00."

Asa thanked her. She left as she arrived, quiet, small, efficient.

Bria shifted her weight and looked at the board with the ring overlay and the Chamber glass photo. "Will your complaint touch their funding," she said.

"It goes to city management first," I said. "Then to the council. They can condition their next allocation on training and controls. They can redirect a portion to the historical society for custodial oversight. They can move nothing. Tonight I am not a vote. I am a clerk."

She nodded. She likes when people say what they can do and stop. So do I.

Nina chewed pastry and then wiped her fingers with a napkin Harold produced from nowhere. She looked at Toby and then down the block at the hall where she has argued a dozen times and won two, which counts. "I do not care if a story sells," she said to no one in particular. "I care if it holds."

Paula heard it and gave her a small half smile, not agreement, not comfort. Respect.

Gran passed the ledger to Asa. He signed the line about the charges and the complaint. He writes like a man who learned to print before schools thought script made you clever. I prefer it.

The board members huddled by the meter. Martin looked at Asa. "May I say one sentence," he said.

"Not tonight," Asa said. "You will have your microphone in a room that is built for microphones. This curb is for chain. We will keep it clean."

Martin swallowed a comment and nodded. He is smart enough to know when a no holds.

A camera from the local station arrived late, caught the tail, and tried to push a mic near Asa's shoulder. He lifted his palm the same way. The reporter looked past him to the board and then to me. I shook my head and pointed at the paper on the truck. She photographed the board through the glass instead and wrote her own notes. I will read her version tomorrow and correct nothing. The wall can take it.

Asa nodded to the uniforms. They stepped in, not rough, not hurried. One at Toby's elbow, one at his far shoulder. They said sir and please and watch your step because they are good at their jobs and have no need to season a night with salt. Toby turned his face toward the bay as he moved. For a second he looked at the counter board, the line across the top that says 6:11 RBK, 6:12 VOID, and the overlay at the bottom where the registry ring holds and the live impression drifts. He looked at the star in the bag.

He took one breath and closed his eyes and let himself be led to the car. He did not fight. He did not speak.

The squad door shut. The light bars kept their slow pulse. A neighbor said she needed to get home to a sitter and left with a quick squeeze of my forearm. Bria went to help Rafi fold the last tablecloth. Harold made sure the pastry bag had emptied to the right hands. Nina stood still for a count, then turned toward the alley and stopped herself with a look at Paula's chair. She sat instead and put her hand flat on the seat like she was holding a lid on a boiling pot. She does that when she chooses sense. It makes a better town.

Gran pressed the ledger closed with both palms and carried it inside. I followed and set the case box on the safe. We locked the safe with a key and a code and wrote the time like clerks do when they want to sleep later. The shop breathed different with the evidence gone. Lighter and emptier. Not cleaner. Clean comes after.

When I stepped back to the doorway, Asa was standing alone with his hands in his pockets and his eyes on the awning. He looked tired, not from lack of sleep, from the kind of day where you hold fifteen truths in your head and keep them from rolling off the table. He looked at me and lifted one eyebrow.

"Good wall," he said. That counts as praise from him. He tapped the door frame with the back of his knuckles and stepped to the car.

"Eat," Gran said behind me, pressing a wedge of pastry into my palm. I took a bite. It tasted like butter and sugar and heat. It tasted like morning. She knows when to hand food to a person who forgot to take care of herself.

Paula picked up a cone and stacked it with the other three and carried the group inside. Rafi killed the projector. The board lost its glow but kept its shape. Peppermint leaped from the bay to the register stool and turned in one circle and settled, nose tucked, eyes half shut. He will sleep where the shop breathes.

The board members came to the door to say something. I held a palm and shook my head. "Tomorrow," I said. "Not tonight."

They nodded and walked toward Oak with their hands in their coat pockets and their heads close together. They will try to write a version that hurts less. The city will read ours.

Tessa, the intern, hung at the back of the crowd and did not step forward. She looked fifteen out there in the spill from the streetlamp. She looked at the tote hooks and then at her hands. I called her name.

"You keep your head," I said. "You come by at ten if you want work."

She nodded a fast nod, like gratitude and fright share a road in her body. She left with small steps.

The last vendor dragged the tent pole to the curb where the city truck would claim it in the morning. He waved a half wave and tucked his chin into his collar. He will be back next month for the bingo night. Town recycles events like plates.

I went to the board and pulled one card to move it half an inch to the left because my eye wanted it that way. Gran watched me and smiled with nothing soft in it. Approval without sugar plays better on my day.

Inside, the shop felt like the shop again. Shelves that sit where they should. A bell that rings when it feels like it. Paper in stacks that do not tip. The vitrine held the wrong stamp under the right acrylic, but that, too, had its line on the docket now.

Asa's last order on the curb sat in my head while I wiped the counter. Lock the pool iPads. Seal the tote supply. Inventory the lanyards. Copier glass for service. Keys on a sign-out form. Event rules on paper with six signatures. Corrective path. It is a list as tidy as any night can ask for. The Chamber will do it if they want to stay in the room where grownups talk.

Paula came back to the door, leaned a shoulder on the jamb, and watched the street empty.

"You going to sleep," she said.

"I am going to put today on a shelf and label it," I said. "Then I will try."

She nodded. "Call if you do not," she said.

"I will," I said.

She left. Gran turned off the over-bay spots. Rafi locked the back. The alley sat quiet. The title office camera blinked a small green in the distance like an eye that does not blink.

I walked to the rare nook and set a card on the case for morning.

Case file, evidence transferred. Charges read. Complaint lodged. Lock audit begins at nine.

Then I stood at the door and looked at the curb. The light bars were gone. The streetlight threw a strong circle with a moth inside it. The people were home. The room had done its work.

We stood in the doorway in a line that makes a town. Gran with the ledger under her arm. Rafi with a roll of tape in his back pocket. Paula with a cone in one hand and a key in the other. Peppermint with his tail draped over the stool rung. Me with pastry sugar on my thumb and ink under my nail. No one spoke.

The circle stands quiet. No speeches.

CHAPTER 20

Shop Reset

Morning clears the glass like a cloth. The street sits plain, washed by a light drizzle that left the curb clean and the smell of wet dust in the air. I open the front door of Peppermint Cat at eight on the dot and breathe in paper, ink, and soap. No lights from patrol. No cluster of faces. Quiet. The way a shop prefers to wake.

Rafi arrives with a roll of blue tape, a canvas tool bag, and a mug that steams. Gran follows with the witness ledger, a folder of clean forms, and the small brass key to the bulletin frame. Paula slips in with a pad, two markers, and a coil of nylon cord. Peppermint trots from the back, checks the threshold, checks me, and accepts that the room belongs to us again.

We do the thing that keeps this place true. We post the rules, we sign the lines, we set the shelf.

I flip the counter lamp to warm and slide a stack of crisp sheets from the tray. Title on top reads Exhibit Handling Rules. Yesterday gave us the proof. Today gives us the guardrails.

I lay the first page on the glass and read it once for tone.

Exhibit Handling Rules

> 1. No off-network devices in event areas. Phones in the lockbox or powered down. Staff and guest devices

connect only to Peppermint Cat Staff. Guest network disabled during exhibits.

2. No unlogged handling. Every touch logs to the Exhibit Ledger with time, purpose, name, and witness. Keys sign out and in on the same line.
3. No unscheduled moves. Vitrines, presses, and cases move on calendar with two signatures and a photo of the start and finish.
4. No external printing for exhibit materials. All cards print in-house on recorded queues. If we need a partner logo, we import the file; we do not import their printer ghosts.
5. No blackout effects. No staged cuts. If a room needs darkness for a slide, we keep the aisles clear and the path taped.
6. No tote-borne tools on the floor. Tools live in the back bench with a checkout card. Free drivers stay in a sealed bin.
7. No Chamber pool devices on our networks without a signed plan and an IP list taped to this board.
8. Any incident at the glass, the case, or the shelf triggers a freeze, a call to me, and a photo. No one cleans until I sign.
9. Two-person rule for the stamp case. Me plus witness. Head never leaves the room without Asa's paper.
10. Event partners sign these rules before we hang a single bunting.

I set the sheet into the bulletin frame, swing it shut, and lock it. Gran signs the frame log beneath the glass with her square hand, witness today, 8:04 a.m. Paula draws a thin border on the wall around the frame with blue tape so the eye lands and stays.

"Router," Rafi says.

I nod. He steps to the office and disables Peppermint Cat Guest from the admin page. He prints the change log and three copies of the network rules. One goes in the binder. One goes inside the bulletin frame behind the rules as an insert. One goes to the back bench to live with the drivers.

We build the handling post next. Paula strings the nylon cord across the front of the Founders table and clips a clean sign in the center.

Please look. Do not touch. Handling by scheduled staff only.

Gran writes the day's opening entry in the Exhibit Ledger.

8:07 a.m., rules posted and signed, Guest network disabled, handling cord set. Witness G. Wren.

"Now the shelf," I say.

The press base is out of here. Evidence. Asa's courier signed it out last night at 10:12. We keep the photo of the new screw on the board as a quiet teacher. The shelf lip shows the driver scrape from the pivot job like a thin white scar. Clearance came at 7:30 a.m. to clean and fill non-evidence surfaces. Rafi unlocks the rare nook and lays out a felt pad, a small block plane, a jar of shellac, a wax stick in a dull gray, two cotton cloths, and a leveling bubble.

He does it slow. We do not erase history; we seal it so it cannot hurt anyone. He takes one pass with the plane to knock the sharp out of the scrape, fills the line with the wax, warms it with a breath, and burns it in with a cotton pad. The fill takes the light the way the rest of the edge takes the light. He rubs a finger across it. Smooth. He wicks a narrow line of shellac along the grain and lets it sit. No shine. No show.

He checks the shelf screws. The old three groan and stop where they should. He leaves them. The hole where the new one lived waits empty; we log it, not patch it. He drops the bubble on the edge. Center. He sets the corner braces, writes their torque on a small tag, and tapes the tag under the lip where only a clerk will look.

"Press placard," Paula says.

I hand her the draft I typed while the coffee ran.

Cast-Iron Book Press
Temporarily removed for inspection and safety review.
Return scheduled after city clearance.
Contact: L. Wren, custodian.

She prints it at twelve point, black on cream, no logos. She slides it into the small holder at the edge of the shelf. People do not need drama. They need straight words.

We move to the case. The vitrine holds the wrong head. No more. I unlock the acrylic. Gran stands next to me with the ledger. Rafi films my hands. I lift the replica with the towel and set it in the evidence box with the sticker ghost card and the live impression we pressed under yesterday's paper. The lid latches with a soft click. I lock the case empty, tip the light to neutral, and set a card dead center under the glass.

Town Ex-Libris Stamp
Removed to secured storage while chain review completes.
Registry card and restoration plate on view by request.

The registry card and the H&K photo live in a separate sleeve in the safe. Today I place a facsimile behind the counter. If a regular asks, I will show the photo under the lamp and then I will close the sleeve and put it away. No touch. No heat.

Gran signs the case log at 8:21. Two names, two times, one line.

The counter needs its own rules where hands land. I lay a smaller card on the glass at the right corner where people set cups.

No drinks on handling glass.
Use coasters at all times.
Thank you.

It is dull and strict and perfect. Paula adds four coasters to the counter from the drawer. Gran smiles. No ring ghosts on our glass, not today.

We hang the last sheet at the back door, eye level with anyone who thinks short cuts belong in alleys.

Back Door Policy
Door remains locked during events.
Smart lock codes restricted to staff. No partner codes.
Alley access by schedule only. Camera logs reviewed daily.

Rafi prints today's camera sync screenshot and tapes it behind the back counter where I can see it if a person asks for a time. Alignment makes a clerk's life easy.

I take a breath and look from frame to frame. Rules under glass. Cord across the table. Shelf smooth and level, tag taped beneath. Case empty and honest. Back door policy plain. Network rules in the binder. Guest network off. No tote of freebies near the bench. The room feels steadier. It is not proud. It is ready.

Gran clears her throat. "The pledge," she says.

We started it in Book Night after the water leak three winters ago. We used it once since. Today earns it. I pull the little placard from the drawer, set it on the counter, and read it out.

We hold firsts and first truths for the town. We do not cut corners for clout. We write it down. We sign our names.

Gran signs the day's line below it. Rafi signs next. Paula signs with that tidy teacher hand. I sign last and slide the card back into the drawer. Ritual belongs to work, not to show.

We open the door at nine. No fanfare. The first two in are a father and a small boy with a gap in his teeth. The boy stops at the cord. He reads the sign aloud, sounds out handling, looks at his father, and nods once like a person who understands the pact. He asks if the cat is on duty. I say he is between tasks and point to Peppermint. Peppermint pretends not to hear. Texture.

Mrs. Aldrin arrives with a canvas bag of paperbacks and a note for the community board. She glances at the empty case and then at me. I give her the plain line she deserves.

"The stamp is secured while we complete the chain review," I say. "You can see the registry photo at the counter if you like."

"I like rules on walls," she says. "They keep the floor safe." She leaves three paperbacks and a jar of plum jam and goes on with her day without asking for a speech.

Bria slides in at 9:20 with coffee filters and a ledger line from last night's Square batch, neat as a pin. She looks at the network rules and gives me a half salute.

"Staff only," she says.

"Staff only," I say.

She taps the tote hook once with the back of her fingers and smiles without softness. The hook is empty. The drivers are in a sealed bin with a card signed on the lid. She approves. She goes to help Rafi check the new torque tags on the shelf and the brace screws on the ladder. She reads the number aloud. He reads the same number aloud. Two voices make one record.

Nina arrives with a rolled poster for her debate night and stops at the bulletin frame.

"No blackouts," she reads. "Say it again."

"No blackouts," I say.

She taps the glass with her nail once. "Good," she says, and pins her poster to the corkboard with one pin at each corner, neat, square, no lean.

Asa steps in at 9:40 with a short sheet from the city manager. It confirms clearance to clean non-evidence surfaces, notes our complaint filing number, and lists the corrective path items he read on the curb. He signs our copy and I tape it inside the bulletin frame behind the rules in case someone wants to ask a foolish question at noon.

"Any fire to put out," he says.

"Only coffee," I say.

He looks at the shelf edge, sees the fill, nods once. He looks at the empty case and the small card and nods again. He does not need a tour. He knows the room when it's right. He signs the Exhibit Ledger as a witness to the morning reset, backs up, and fades.

A man from the title office walks across with an envelope. Annie sent over a flash drive copy of the alley slice and a signed chain cover. He hands it to me like a neighbor handing over sugar. The town knows how to pass a thing without heat. I thank him, file it, and set a sticky on the safe with the time and my initials.

Paula moves through the floor like a seamstress. She lifts a chair one inch and sets it back down. She pulls the cord taut and ties a second knot. She taps a cone to check for wobble and rotates it a hair. She adds a rule to the Volunteer Guide with a pen.

Volunteer Guide, addendum:

- Direct donors to staff for exhibit questions.
- Keep totes off the floor. If you need a pen, ask.
- If you hear a chime, freeze and look for me.

Clear. No fluff. She draws a box around it and tapes the guide to the inside of the back door. People read what lives where their hands land.

I take one last walk to the office. The public workstation sits under the window, browser history cleared, profile reset, printer queue empty. Rafi taped a small card to the monitor bezel that reads Shared Box. No carts. No checkouts. If a partner wants a cart, we print it. They do not touch this keyboard. I like the look of that card.

I pull a fresh handling kit for the day: cotton gloves, lint cloth, small scale, date card, pen, and two sleeves. It lives in a shallow tray under the counter now, not three steps away. We learned what distance costs. I slide the tray into the slot and close the drawer. The click sounds like a note at the end of a measure.

At ten Gran brings out the Founders Ledger and sets it on the easel near the cord. Not to display the guts, to show the spine. She hangs a small sign above it.

View by staff turn only. Ask. We will show you our proof.

People will. We will. No drama.

A pair from the historical society stops by to say the board voted to offer oversight on the Chamber's artifact program until their review finishes. They have a standard form and a clean seal. I sign a simple acknowledgment that our shop welcomes their training schedule and will sit the first class. Gran signs as custodian. Paula signs as volunteer lead. Rafi signs as bench lead. We do not roll our eyes. Training is not an insult. Training is a favor you choose to take.

At ten thirty, Rafi resets the travel aisle wax. He cones the ends, sets a small card on the shelf that reads Wet Finish, checks the timer, and steps back while it cures. He practices his own rules. No one lifts a cone without his hand on it.

Peppermint does a slow patrol, stops at the cord, tests it with one paw, deems it not worth playing with, and heads for the moderator's chair. He leaps, turns once, and drops on the cushion with a sigh and a crooked paw. He closes one eye, then the other, then both. The chair belongs to him until noon.

A few town faces drift in. The janitor with the smiley K peers in, gives me a nod, and walks on. The board member who tried to speak last night walks in with his hands open. He reads the rules in the frame, reads the back door policy, looks at the empty case, looks at me, and says nothing. Good. He leaves a donation at the counter and signs his name in the daily ledger. He does not ask for a receipt. We give him one anyway. Paula stamps it with the little cat.

By eleven, the day feels like it belongs to the shop again. I pull a single card from the case file and write the final entry for this book with a fresh pen. I keep the sentences small, the way a line sits on a label.

Card, 11:02 a.m.

Exhibit rules posted. Guest network disabled. Shelf edge filled and leveled. Case emptied and logged. Founders Ledger view by request. Drivers sealed. Tote hook clear. Back door policy hung. Staff and volunteers signed. City clearance taped. Training scheduled.

I tuck the card into the binder at the front, next to the two-up we printed of the live impression and the sticker ghost. I close the rings and listen for the note. There it is.

Gran comes to the counter, taps the bulletin frame once with the back of her hand, and nods to the room.

"Proof on the walls tends to keep hands honest," she says.

"Proof on the walls keeps me honest," I say.

She gives me the look she saves for when I get close to sentimental and do not deserve a pass. I swallow a smile and check the clock.

Paula brings a small stack of laminated copies of the rules for event partners to sign. She has already punched holes for a binder. There is a satisfaction in that kind of foresight. She is a teacher. The world is better with more of them.

Rafi slides a torque driver into the bench drawer and puts a checkout card on top of it.

Small flat, 5.5. Card line reads: borrowed by, purpose, time out, time in, witness. He will scowl the first time someone tries to leave the card blank. I will back him. We learned how light a driver feels in the hand and how heavy a driver feels on a shelf when the marks it makes show in court.

The bell rings and a courier drops a padded envelope at the counter. Inside, the H&K technician's archived plates we requested yesterday. I show Gran the mark at ring ten and the ear flat in the lab print and slide the plate into a sleeve behind the registry photo. We have what we need to put a small sign on the case when the head returns.

Public record available. Ask to see the registry and the plate.

We will not show it to every passerby. We will show it when the question deserves the ink.

At noon, Asa texts one line. Board accepted the corrective path as read. Pool iPads locked. Lanyards inventoried. Drivers boxed. Copier glass cleaned. I tape the print of that text behind the rules inside the frame with a small note.

Partner compliance at 12:02 p.m.

No one will clap. They will see it, and some will sleep better.

I stand at the threshold and look across the floor. The Founders table looks like a place to learn, not a place to pose. The cord says look, not lean. The case says honest. The shelf says safe. The board says no blackouts. The door says do your work in the open.

Peppermint snores once and then sinks deeper into the chair with one paw over his nose. Gran uses a soft brush to lift a thread from the corner of the bulletin frame. Rafi writes a small tag for the ladder brace with the torque number and the day. Paula circles a date on the volunteer calendar and writes Training Day in a blocky hand.

We did not fix the world. We locked our room to the standard we claim we serve. That is enough for a morning.

I pick up the pen and write the last line on the case card for myself, for Gran, for anyone who reads the spine later when some new mess tries to edge in.

Firsts matter. So does first truth. We keep both clean.

END OF BOOK ONE

PEPPERMINT CAT BOOKSHOP MYSTERIES

ABOUT THE AUTHOR

Ivy Grant is a celebrated fiction author best known for her gripping mysteries and heart-racing adventure novels that blend sharp intellect with atmospheric storytelling. Born in a quiet coastal town where fog rolled in like secrets, Ivy grew up with a fascination for hidden things—locked drawers, whispered rumors, and maps that didn't quite match the terrain.

Ivy remains famously private, rarely giving interviews and preferring to let her characters do the talking. When she's not writing, she's said to be hiking through storm-lashed moors, sketching story ideas on café napkins, or cataloging antique keys she insists will someday open something extraordinary.

THANK YOU.

Printed in Dunstable, United Kingdom